A Diamond for Christmas

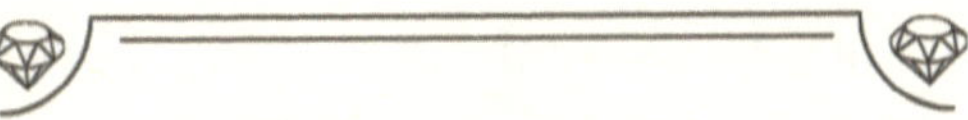

Diamonds of the First Water
Prequel

SYDNEY JANE BAILY

cat whisker press

Boston

DIAMONDS OF THE FIRST WATER

A Diamond for Christmas

Clarity

Purity

Adam

Radiance

Brilliance

OTHER WORKS

The RAKES ON THE RUN Series
Last Dance in London
Pursued in Paris
Banished to Brighton
Gretna Green by Sunset
The Lady Who Stole Christmas

The RARE CONFECTIONERY Series
The Duchess of Chocolate
The Toffee Heiress
My Lady Marzipan
The Gingerbread Lady

The DEFIANT HEARTS Series
An Improper Situation
An Irresistible Temptation
An Inescapable Attraction
An Inconceivable Deception
An Intriguing Proposition
An Impassioned Redemption

The BEASTLY LORDS Series
Lord Despair
Lord Anguish
Lord Vile
Lord Darkness
Lord Misery
Lord Wrath
Lord Corsair
Eleanor

PRESENTING LADY GUS

THE BLACK KNIGHT'S REWARD
with Marliss Melton

DEDICATION

To those who love fiercely
and bravely

INTRODUCTION TO
DIAMONDS OF THE FIRST WATER

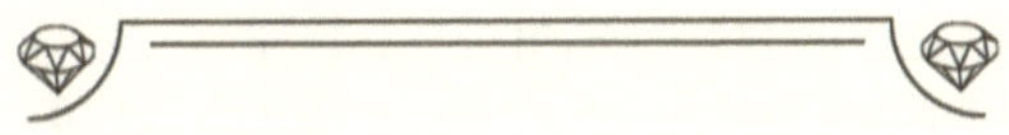

Once upon a time, an Irish family by the name of O'Diamáin emigrated to England from the north of Ireland, from County Doire to be specific. You may know the area as Derry or even Londonderry if you are thinking of it after King James I granted the city a royal charter.

Felim O'Diamáin, who was the youngest son, sailed across the Irish Sea to make his fortune, bringing his pretty wife and two young children with him. As the story goes, they stopped over on the Isle of Man for a perfectly peaceful night before landing at Ravenglass the next day and traipsing through the Lake District.

Another version swears they took the shorter but far more dangerous route north across the sea to Portpatrick, finding themselves in the southernmost part of Scotland. From there, if they indeed came that way, they headed east toward Gretna Green. Not for any quick anvil marriage, mind you, but to traverse the border to England.

No one knows for sure the veracity of either tale, nor particularly cares. Once they arrived in England, Felim did very well for himself, as did his descendants.

At some point during the twelve-year reign of George I, another O'Diamáin by the name of Liam was made an earl for his devoted service to the Crown. During those years in the early eighteenth century, King George also created a few dukes, at least one marquess, some barons, a single viscount, and other earls. But we're not interested in any of them, although some may have helped to quell the riots that ensued when Hanoverian George outmaneuvered any pesky residual Stuarts hoping to claim the English throne.

Nevertheless, our interest lies with Liam. With his new earldom came much wealth and land, specifically in Derbyshire. And naturally, a title. However, George I, being of Germanic descent, didn't find the Celtic name of O'Diamáin tripped easily off his tongue. Neither did he master Gaelic or Manx, for that matter. In any case, with a little persuasion and an extra thousand acres, Liam became William, the Earl Diamond, as his male descendants have been known ever since.

Over the years, the earls have enlarged the original house to be an impressive manor, always named Oak Grove Hall, which is the translation of their long-ago home of County *Doire*.

Generations later, as the heir to the earldom and all its assets, Lord Geoffrey Diamond seeks a wife.

CHAPTER ONE

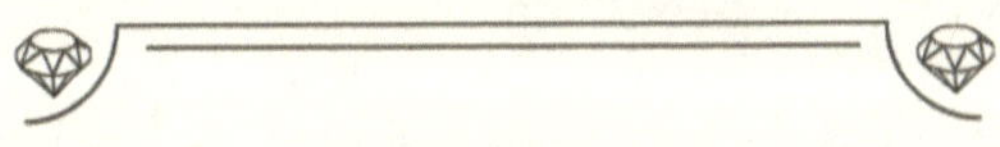

Mayfair, 1824

O *f all the clumsy, imbecilic things to do!* And in front of a
lovely lady, no less. Geoffrey had tripped over the
cellist's chair leg and nearly bumped into a pretty blonde.

"Terribly sorry," he said when the musicians beside him
turned as one to glower while not missing a note of the
mazurka quadrille they were playing. And quite loudly in his
ear, too. But he wasn't apologizing to them, rather to the
vision in blue.

However, she gave him a withering look, not the warm
one he'd hoped for when deciding to go in her direction.
Having been introduced earlier, Geoffrey fully intended to
ask for a dance.

Lifting her chin, the lady strolled past him to take
another man's hand.

Still looking back at her shapely figure, Geoffrey crashed
into another guest.

"Ow!" came a female voice from the vicinity of his cravat
where her face was now pressed.

"Terribly sorry," he repeated, holding her by the
shoulders so she wouldn't tumble backward. All he could
see was the top of her head. It was a view of fiery, copper-
haired coils and an aigrette of small emeralds, which

anchored two peacock feathers tucked alongside her chignon.

Holding her still, he stepped back. When the lady's green gaze locked with his, Geoffrey was reminded of his family's verdant Derbyshire estate.

"No harm done, my lord," she said, offering a smile that stole his breath.

"Who *are* you?" he asked, mesmerized. At the same time, the performers enthusiastically played a crescendo.

Frowning, she asked, "Into the garden?"

That couldn't be what the red-headed young woman said, not unless she was the most forward lady at Lord and Lady Fenwick's Belgrave Square ball.

Bending low, he put his ear close to her pink-tinged, satiny lips.

"I said, 'I beg your pardon,'" she clarified.

Then he put his own mouth to the delicate shell of her ear.

"I asked your name," he explained.

She reared back and looked up at him. As the musicians now played less enthusiastically, he could hear her next words.

"You are breaking rules right and left," she told him, entirely without animosity. In fact, she seemed entertained. "You know you cannot ask me that question, not in such an informal manner."

"Of course not!" he agreed, glad she wasn't annoyed. He needed a formal introduction. *What on earth was wrong with him?*

Yet never having seen her before at any assembly, Geoffrey feared she would vanish before he could discover her identity.

"And your hands are still upon me," she reminded him, having to speak loudly over the music.

Yes, they were. And under his gloved fingers, she was warm and soft. He didn't wish to release her, but he did.

"Stay there," Geoffrey ordered. "Don't move."

Her eyes widened.

"If you wouldn't mind," he added.

Looking around wildly, he spotted their host walking in the opposite direction.

"Lord Fenwick," he exclaimed. Then he looked at the coppery goddess. "I shall return with our host at once."

Sprinting in the direction of the old viscount, Geoffrey managed to catch him before he left the room, going so far as to grab his father's friend by the arm.

"My lord, if you would be so kind as to introduce me to a female so I may ask her to dance, I would greatly appreciate it."

"Diamond," the man greeted him. "Searching for a wife at last, are you?"

At last? Geoffrey wasn't ancient! At twenty-six, he considered himself the perfect age.

"Hoping for a new bride by Christmas?" Lord Fenwick continued. "That would make your parents happy, no doubt."

"No, my lord. I mean, yes, I would like to marry, but not in haste."

"Right you are. Marry in haste, repent in leisure, as they say."

"Exactly," Geoffrey agreed. "Would you mind introducing me to a fetching lady whom I've never seen before?"

"Naturally, I shall."

Geoffrey turned, peering across the room to where he'd left her, but she was no longer there.

"She's gone!" he exclaimed, experiencing keen disappointment.

"Who is?" the viscount asked.

Geoffrey sighed. "I don't know her name, my lord. I shall go find her again."

"Don't let her get away," Lord Fenwick called after him, making other heads turn.

Geoffrey would be the laughingstock of this springtime ball.

CAROLINE WISHED THE DASHING, dark-haired man would come back before her mother or her aunt spied her. Alas, within a few seconds of the stranger's departure, her mother noticed she hadn't returned from speaking with a friend. Lady Chimes, with her sister beside her, came to collect her only daughter.

"Why are you standing like a fence post?" her mother asked.

"I am waiting for a handsome man," Caroline replied.

Her aunt smiled, but her mother did not.

"I am certain you shall better capture a man, handsome or otherwise, by dancing with him rather than by standing next to the musicians. Come along, Caroline. I have the very nobleman in mind for you. He was just introduced to us by our host."

Caroline was unceremoniously dragged away to meet some Lord Nit-Wit. Sadly, although the new man was also a stranger, he wasn't the one who had placed his hands upon her shoulders, making her tingle. He wasn't the one with dark hair and deep blue eyes the color of delphiniums, nor the one who smelled deliciously of sandalwood and Pears soap, the same as her family used.

He had crashed into her and then held on, and every part of her had cried out for him never to let go. It was the strangest, most delightfully overwhelming sensation she'd ever experienced.

She danced a quadrille with the young man whose name she'd instantly forgotten while wishing she'd learned the name of the man whom she would not soon forget.

And then she saw him, standing by a towering candelabra, surveying the dance floor. She had the strangest inkling he was searching for her.

Sure enough, when his blue gaze landed upon her, he smiled, and it lit up his entire face. He even took a step onto the dance floor and was nearly run over by two couples before he hurried to the side again.

He was as enthusiastic as a puppy, yet as alluring as a sable-haired wolf.

"Lady Caroline," came the voice of her partner.

She had faltered and made a misstep while making moon-eyes across the room.

"I apologize." She wanted to ask if they could stop, but it would ruin the formation for the other three couples in their group, so she persevered. As soon as the music ended, Caroline let her partner escort her back to her mother and aunt, who had come to the ball to keep them company as they often did.

A moment later, her blue-eyed stranger appeared before them. Beside him were their evening's hosts, both Lord and Lady Fenwick, who addressed her mother first.

"Lady Chimes, may we introduce the son of an acquaintance of ours?"

Lydia Chimes smiled to their hosts and to the broad-shouldered young man, letting her hazel glance slide over him. When she turned her mouth up, Caroline's mother looked like a young lady herself and had not a streak of gray in her red hair, a shade darker than her daughter's.

"Why, yes," her mother said. "If he and his family are known to you, then I am sure we would be delighted to meet him."

"Good, good," Lord Fenwick said. "Lady Chimes, this is Lord Diamond. His father is—"

"I know who his father is," Caroline's mother interrupted, and the change in her was as unexpected as it was swift. "And his mother, too."

Caroline gawked at her harsh tone, having never heard the like in public and rarely in private, either. She glanced at her aunt for an explanation, but Aunt Cordelia merely shook her head. Apparently, she knew what this was about.

Lady Fenwick frowned, obviously not enjoying any discord at her ball. However, not catching the import of Lady Chimes's words, Lord Fenwick continued, "Well, that's fine, then. Lord Geoffrey was under the impression you were both unknown to him and sought me out to make an introduction."

"We have no interest in making this man's acquaintance," her mother added with a voice as chilly as ice.

"Mother," Caroline said softly, wishing she could recant Lady Chimes's rudeness. She would not dare to gainsay her in front of others, even as she watched a puzzled expression cross over Lord Diamond's face. At least now she knew his name.

"His mother, I shall not discuss, but his father is a dishonorable man," Lady Chimes continued, "and thus, I can only assume *his son* is as well."

"My lady, I assure you—" Lord Diamond began.

"You shall not assure me of anything, young man," Caroline's mother said before addressing their hosts again. "I have been dreading such an occurrence, of coming across a Diamond whilst at an event, ever since we moved back from Bath. And now it has happened, and me without my husband by my side for strength."

Caroline managed to stop herself from rolling her eyes while her aunt raised an eyebrow of incredulity. After all, the fierce Lady Chimes was every bit as formidable as Lord Chimes. In some instances, more so.

"Frankly, Lord Fenwick, I'm dismayed this happened at *your* ball." Then her mother turned to her. "Caroline, come along. We shall leave at once."

"Please do not leave on my account," Lord Diamond said, his tone now one of bewilderment.

Caroline felt bad for him, trying to make eye contact, hoping he realized she was as confounded as he was.

"Don't leave upon *any* account," Lord Fenwick entreated. "You three ladies are most welcome to remain."

Her mother lifted her chin and looked away.

"I shall be the one to leave, of course," Lord Diamond said. "I wish I knew what this is about," he told Lady Chimes's shoulder.

Caroline could have died of mortification when her mother continued to ignore him.

Then he looked directly into Caroline's eyes again, and something undeniable passed between them. She believed it was a promise that they would meet again.

Then he turned to their hosts. "While I am befuddled by this lady's accusations, I will not remain and make her uncomfortable. Thank you for inviting me, my lord."

With that, he nodded, bowed shallowly, again to her mother's averted form, to Caroline's aunt, and to her before he strode away.

CHAPTER TWO

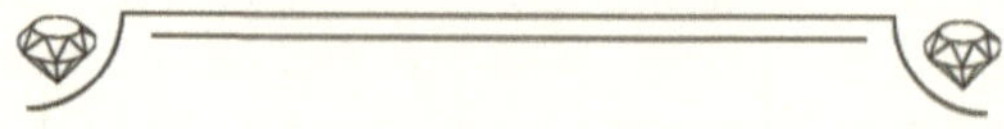

Geoffrey had never heard of the blasted Chimes family before, but now he intended to know everything he could. He'd done the only gentlemanly thing he could think of in the impossibly awkward situation. Nevertheless, he vowed to see Lady Caroline again.

Even if her mother guarded the castle door like a fire-breathing dragon. A red-headed one at that. Speaking of mothers, his own was no shrinking violet.

"Mother!" he called out as soon as he arrived at his parents' townhouse on Hanover Square the following morning. If he wished, he would have inherited it and lived out his days there in later life, except he'd found a residence more in the thick of things on Piccadilly where he intended to raise a family.

Their butler, Mr. Fogerty, didn't mind when he showed himself into the drawing room to wait.

"Geoffrey," Lady Marianne Diamond greeted, sweeping in on her satin-slippered feet. "How wonderful of you to visit but how dreadfully naughty. It's frightfully early. The sun is barely up," she declared, even though it had gone half-past nine. "Fogerty, bring me a cup of chocolate as soon as you possibly can."

"Yes, my lady. And for you, my lord?" he addressed Geoffrey, who hadn't lived there for going on three years.

"Coffee," Geoffrey said. "With cream. Thank you, Fogerty."

When the man had gone, Geoffrey turned to his mother, who had seated herself upon the gold velvet sofa.

"What can you tell me of the Chimes family, and why do they hate us?"

He had her attention at the mention of the family's name.

"Hate us?" She sniffed, then sighed and looked at her nails, plainly stalling.

"Yes, you know them. I can see that."

"Don't tell me the frightful Lady Chimes has come back from Bath and brought her handsome, beleaguered husband with her? It was so pleasant knowing that family was on the other side of England. I suppose she made a scene. She is the lowest mushroom I can imagine. I don't know how Lord Chimes puts up with her."

Geoffrey narrowed his eyes. And then, thinking of his mother's wild youth, considered the most sought-after young lady at the turn of the century, a favorite at King George's court, he could guess she was involved.

"What did *you* do to them?" he asked.

"Me?" She was all blue-eyed innocence.

"Yes, you." He took a seat, determined to hear the *whys* and the *hows* of it.

"Why does everyone always think I am responsible when things go badly? Your father used to say I caused those three big stones to fall over at Stonehenge."

"No, Mother, that was due to frost and happened a long time ago. More recently, if you recall, you caused Lord Spiren to leave Lady Spiren."

Her nostrils flared. "It was not my fault the man became entirely besotted with me."

"Perhaps. Perhaps not." His mother was an unconscionable flirt.

"You are my son, and I will not be interrogated by you," Lady Diamond declared.

After the chocolate and coffee were served, Geoffrey tried again. "I only want to know why Lady Chimes wouldn't accept a simple introduction from me. Although come to think of it, she said Father had no honor, not you."

Instead of being bothered by a slight against her husband, his mother shrugged.

"Coming from a mushroom," she muttered.

"An attractive one," he said, trying to learn the truth, all fiery hair and green eyes like her beautiful daughter. "Did Father love her very much?"

"*Pish,*"his mother said, and the story came from her lips like water from a fountain. "It's the other way around. Lord Chimes adored me, but your father enticed me away from him. She's simply annoyed at being chosen second. She knows if her husband could have had me, she would have ended up some obscure baronet's wife, or worse, instead of a countess."

Geoffrey stirred his coffee. "Are you telling me on behalf of her jealous husband, she considers *my* father dishonorable? That's unlikely. After all, Lord Chimes's loss of you was her gain."

His mother sipped her chocolate. "There may have been something else."

"May have been?" Geoffrey prompted.

"Your father *may* have placed a wager with Lord Chimes and against all odds won, thereby draining the other man's coffers a little. I don't think the money mattered. It was the issue of the wager, which I never did suss out."

Geoffrey sighed. His mother liked to dance and batt her eyelashes and sing, too, whenever asked, and his father liked to laugh and occasionally to gamble. Mostly, they were both harmless since his mother never took her flirtation too far, and his father usually came out on top. *But, still!*

"Anyway," his mother asked, "why do you care if you are introduced to Lady Chimes? She's a bit long in the tooth for you, dear son of mine." Her familiar, ready laughter erupted.

He didn't feel like laughing.

"I wanted to dance with her daughter."

Lady Diamond perked up. "Don't even think it."

"Mother, you don't know the Chimes's daughter."

"True, and you don't either. Only think how she could exact revenge upon her parents' behalf. She might lead you on simply to break your heart. Or worse, lead you down the garden path to ensure a proposal. The idea of being linked through marriage to Lord and Lady Chimes is absolutely out of the question."

"I wouldn't mind," he said, thinking again how lovely Lady Caroline was and how sweet her lips.

"Not *you*! Us!" she said. "Your father and I could hardly invite them over for supper, could we? It would be excruciating."

"Liable to end in a duel if you behaved as your normal self," Geoffrey suggested.

"Preposterous," his mother said. Then added, "But entirely likely. Thus, the answer is no, no, no!"

"I wasn't asking your permission," Geoffrey reminded her. He would dance with, kiss, and marry whomever he damn well pleased.

His mother rolled her eyes. "Never mind. I don't need to do anything to stop this carriage wreck. Lord and Lady Chimes won't let you within a furlong of their precious daughter. Mark my words."

"Why won't you tell me?" Caroline demanded of her mother as soon as the ball ended, and they were in their carriage, on the way home to Upper Brook Street near Grosvenor Gate. Her parents had purchased the residence upon returning from fifteen years in Bath.

Her mother had refused to speak of the Diamonds at all. But her aunt raised a single perfectly auburn eyebrow, and

Caroline knew she would find her answers the following day.

Thus, taking her maid, Caroline went directly to the home of her mother's sister at the polite hour of two o'clock. If they hadn't been out late at the ball, then she might have gone at regular visiting hours, beginning at eleven, but she knew Aunt Cordelia wouldn't have yet awakened.

As it was, her aunt, while still wearing her dressing gown and house slippers, invited Caroline upstairs to her bedchamber.

"We'll take tea in here," Cordelia told her maid, and they sat on the soft, blue velvet chairs by her aunt's window overlooking Berkeley Square. "You want to know about that dash-fire, Diamond, don't you?"

Caroline smiled. "Yes!"

"What a family!" her aunt exclaimed.

"Tell me," Caroline insisted.

"His mother was a stunner. She still is, I would warrant, although I haven't seen her in ages. She caught your father's eye, along with every man's, in her first year out in society. My sister saw it all. You know she loved your father at first sight but was too shy to tell him."

"My mother . . . shy?" Caroline mused.

"You become more of a tiger with age, dear girl, especially after having children. You and your two brothers are her whole life. And your father's, too, of course."

Caroline contemplated her mother as a young, unsure woman. It was hard to do.

"So, Father fell for Lady Diamond—"

"*Before* she was Lady Diamond," her aunt reminded her. "It was anyone's guess whose lady she would become. I believe for a little while, your father thought she would become *his* Lady Chimes. And then Diamond decided he wanted her for himself. I believe he secured her by compromising her. A little scandal brewed, and then suddenly, they had announced their engagement."

"Really!" Caroline's imagination took flight. After having gazed into the younger Diamond's blue eyes, she could well believe he might get her into a compromising situation with a crook of his finger.

On the other hand, what if it had been a forced marriage? "Maybe Lady Diamond really loved *my* father but had to marry Lord Diamond," Caroline considered.

Her aunt wrinkled her nose and shook her head. "I think she knew exactly what she was doing and whom she wanted. In any case, with her out of the way, your father noticed your mother. And that, as they say, was that."

"And my mother disapproves of Lord Diamond because of his rakish behavior with Lady Diamond?" Caroline asked. "That seems absurd, considering he cleared the way for Father to be with Mother."

"I think my dear sister states that she dislikes Lord Diamond but is actually still a bit green at the gills over *Lady* Diamond, although she shouldn't be. Your father was absolutely besotted with your mother from their first dance, and he's been a devoted husband ever since."

"I know," Caroline agreed with a nod. "I've seen evidence of their love many times over the years. Just the way they look at one another."

"Precisely," her aunt said.

"And does Father dislike the Diamonds, too?"

Aunt Cordelia sipped her tea. "Lord Diamond and your father both belong to White's. There was a wager. Diamond won."

"Oh dear," Caroline said. Her father hated to lose.

"Some said Diamond cheated."

"At least now I understand why Mother thinks him dishonorable." And maybe she was correct. "And thus, she'll never let me have an introduction to his son."

"It is highly unlikely," her aunt agreed.

"But did you see his lovely eyes, Auntie? And his face? And his mouth? And his hair?" Caroline couldn't contain her enthusiasm.

"Yes, and his height and the breadth of shoulders, too." Her Aunt Cordelia wore a smile. "A strapping man, to be sure. Regardless, I believe your parents stayed in Bath longer than they'd intended purposefully to keep you out of certain circles of society so you wouldn't run into that particular Diamond heir. And your trip abroad during last year's Season kept you out of harm's way."

Her aunt paused, looking unsure, but then she blurted, "Also the reason why your parents have all but promised you to Lord Mangue."

Caroline set down her teacup with a shaking hand.

"They wouldn't. They haven't!"

"I hoped you were aware," Aunt Cordelia said, "but since you hadn't mentioned it, I wasn't certain."

Shaking her head, Caroline could not credit her aunt's words.

"This isn't the eighteenth century. I do not believe my parents would force me to marry a man I don't know or love."

"But you *do* know him. I've seen you dance twice with him. At the Fenwicks' ball and the one before."

Caroline frowned. "Which man? The tall baron with those unbearably large ears, or the stocky viscount with a single eyebrow stretching across his forehead? Not that looks are the only thing, but sadly, neither man made any further impression upon me besides those unfortunate traits. Certainly not with their humor, nor clever conversation."

"Mangue is the eyebrowed viscount," her aunt confirmed. "And you don't know anything more about Diamond except his looks, either."

"But I wish to," Caroline insisted. "And I intend to. That's the difference. When Diamond stumbled into me, I vow lightning zigzagged throughout my body. His eyes held mine, and there was a kindred spirit."

"Kindred spirit or merely ardent desire for the opposite gender?"

Caroline wasn't shocked at her aunt's question. Certainly, she had felt a wave of yearning for Lord Geoffrey Diamond, but it wasn't solely due to his looks. If it were, then she would feel desire for every good-looking male whom she came across.

"Eyebrow or not, Auntie, I refuse to be forced."

Cordelia sighed. "I believe Lord Mangue is merely a secondary plan in case you don't find someone suitable by yourself. However, if you make a move toward young Diamond, perhaps accepting a dance, you are likely to find yourself engaged to Mangue with a contract signed before the last notes of the quadrille fade away."

"Will you help me? You are my favorite aunt, after all."

"Naughty girl, I am your only aunt, but you know I'll help. I am all for true love, as you know."

Her aunt had been widowed during the Battle of Waterloo when her husband, a captain and one of Wellington's officers, was mortally wounded. She'd never remarried but kept company with some very distinguished gentlemen, nonetheless.

"I do know," Caroline said, smiling fondly at her. "What's more, I hope you find it again yourself."

"You are a good girl for saying so." Aunt Cordelia's cheeks turned a little pink. "Let us focus upon you though, shall we?"

"How do you mean?" Caroline sipped her tea and pushed thoughts of Lord Mangue aside.

"Knowing you would visit me today, I scoured last night's and this morning's papers. It seems young Geoffrey Diamond—"

"Geoffrey," Caroline repeated. "That's a strong yet kind name, isn't it? Geoffrey Diamond. It suits him."

Her aunt sniffed. "I'm surprised you haven't tried out your own name with his yet."

She felt her cheeks grow warm, recalling lying in bed the night before, thinking she liked the resonance of *Lady*

Caroline Diamond, repeating it more than once aloud. It had a romantic but steady character.

"Go on," she urged her aunt. "You were saying."

"Lord Diamond hasn't been much out in society until recently. His showing up at the Fenwicks' home has caused something of a stir, especially when he left so abruptly. That gave him an added layer of mystery. If he was a few years younger, I would say he only wants to dillydally, dance with pretty ladies, and perhaps kiss a few, too. Anything else, we couldn't even discuss. Yet at his age, it can only mean he's ready to find a wife."

"That seems like quite a lot to infer from a single ball," Caroline said, although she couldn't help thinking of the kissing as well as the "anything else" which they couldn't discuss.

Aunt Cordelia shrugged. "Trust me. And trust *The Times!*"

"Even if Lord Diamond is looking for a wife, and even if I wished to discover whether I wanted to be the one for him, what good does that do me when I cannot get near the man?"

"I can almost hear my late husband talking about plans of attack," her aunt said. "We need to maneuver you into close proximity. You simply must attend the next ball at which Diamond may appear, then send an introductory volley over his right flank."

They both chuckled.

Her aunt continued, "And you will need me by your side to permit this perilous mission, rather than my dear sister, who will forbid it."

Caroline's eyes widened. "You would do that?"

"As long as you promise not to do anything rash," Aunt Cordelia said. "Simply dance with the man, see if you fancy him, and then we'll worry about what comes next."

CHAPTER THREE

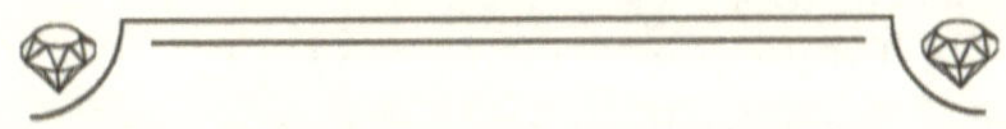

Geoffrey had made it extremely clear to anyone who asked that he would attend Lady Plain de Ville's ball. He'd mentioned it to his tailor so his peers would know, to his butler and housekeeper, so the news would make it through the servant's grapevine, and lastly, to his parents. If Lady Caroline appeared, then she had been forewarned. He hoped he'd seen something in her eyes that bespoke an interest in getting to know him, despite her mother forbidding any such occurrence.

And if Lady Caroline wasn't at the ball, then he would take notice of the lovely ladies who were. He hoped one of them would be as alluring. One of them might make his heart speed up and take his breath away while causing that randy tightening in his loins that the mere sight of the red-headed beauty had produced.

When he entered the ballroom on the second floor of the grand house on Cowley Street, he knew within minutes she wasn't there. Her flame-colored hair would be easy to spot, as well as the glow he seemed to recall emanating from her.

But that was probably only in his imagination.

He greeted the hostess and then began to make his way around the room, chatting with friends, gathering well wishes to give to his parents, and being introduced to a few females with whom he thought it might be pleasant to dance.

In the midst of the Grand March, he saw her enter wearing vivid green silk that set off her fiery locks to perfection. On the other hand, he couldn't think of what color wouldn't. He easily pictured her in scarlet, in saffron, in sapphire blue, and even in black—looking equally stunning. Naturally, his brain added a vivid image of how perfectly spectacular naked as a needle against his cream-colored sheets, too.

She strolled the side of the room with the other woman he recalled from the Fenwicks' ball. He didn't know who she was, but she was definitely not the prickly mother. His luck was changing.

"Careful, my lord," came the warning voice of his partner as he missed a turn.

"My apologies," Geoffrey said and tried to keep his mind on finishing the dance with the lady at hand.

When he left the floor, however, and returned her to her chaperone, Lady Caroline was on the opposite side of the room. Worse, Lady Plain de Ville was introducing her to another man with whom she partnered for the next quadrille.

God's teeth! Geoffrey refrained from asking another lady to dance, as he wouldn't risk laying claim to Lady Caroline a second time. To that end, he approached Lady Plain de Ville.

"Will you make an introduction for me upon the dance's end? I would very much like to meet Lady Caroline," he confessed.

"Certainly," their hostess agreed. Yet she smirked. "Given your two families' histories, I shall be surprised indeed if anything comes of it."

Geoffrey was taken aback. It seemed nobility of a certain age knew about his mother and Lord Chimes or maybe about his father's wager with the man. Either way, it didn't bode well.

"I merely wish to dance with her."

"She is a lovely girl," Lady Plain de Ville said. And then they waited for the interminable quadrille to come to a conclusion.

"Shall we?" their hostess asked.

Together, they intercepted Lady Caroline and her dance partner.

Geoffrey was thrilled to see the lady's ready smile upon seeing him. If he was interpreting correctly, they shared a mutual attraction. For his part, he knew he had a large, foolish grin on his face, and he tried to quell it.

"Lady Caroline, this is Lord Diamond," Lady Plain de Ville got right to the point. "His father is the Earl Diamond. No other family name, as I recall. Most unusual to have the title and the family name be the same, but there you are."

Geoffrey barely heard her prattle. He took Lady Caroline's gloved hand and bowed over it.

"I am enchanting," he said.

As soon as the last word left his lips and he lifted his head, seeing her start to chuckle, he realized his error.

What turned him into a dunderhead around this woman? No one would ever accuse him of being a smooth rogue.

Even Lady Plain de Ville was snickering.

"Well done, my boy," she said and wandered off to tend to her other guests.

"My apologies," Geoffrey said, "but at least I didn't almost knock you over this time."

"You still have hold of my hand," she pointed out, with her perfect lips and soft voice. Not to mention sparkling eyes like sunlit dappled leaves staring into his.

"I do, don't I? And I shall release it," he promised, "as soon as you agree to grant me the honor of the next dance."

"Yes," she agreed.

However, since a dance had begun, he had to release her until a new one began. *What could they do in the meantime?*

"Shall we see if there is any punch or lemonade set out yet?"

"That would be lovely."

They left the ballroom and strolled toward the refreshments in the salon across the hall. A throng of others were already jostling by the serving table.

"I noticed your mother did not accompany you," he said, hoping it wasn't a mistake to bring up the woman who wouldn't even acknowledge him.

"My parents had tickets to the theatre. Thus, Mrs. Waycott, my mother's sister, brought me. Come to think of it, I should have taken you directly to meet her."

He couldn't help his expression of dread as they shuffled closer to the punch bowls.

"Do not worry, my lord," she said, mirth dancing across her face. "My aunt does not hold the same views as my parents."

"That's a relief," he said, handing her a full glass, which was nearly bumped from his grasp by a careless swell.

Snagging another for himself, they moved to the other corner of the room.

"After all," he added, wondering if Lady Caroline knew that both his parents seemed to have strained relationships with hers, "I am not my father, nor my mother."

"I understand," she said.

They spoke no more about it. Instead, he asked her about her life in Bath. She asked him what he'd studied at Oxford. Then, as oft happened, she asked him about his unusual family name, which he explained briefly since the hubbub was loud around them.

"Yet the king couldn't—or wouldn't—pronounce O'Diamáin," he finished. "Which gained us an extra-large land holding in 1717 in exchange for anglicizing our surname. And now, it's time for our dance," he reminded her.

Geoffrey had never enjoyed a dance more, nor a partner. He was as comfortable with Lady Caroline as if he'd known her for ages. At the same time, he relished the new sensations coursing through him—an intense awareness of wherever they touched. With heady desire sparking in his veins, he ached to be alone with her, without any idea how to make that happen.

The dance ended sooner than he could have imagined.

"Will you escort me back to my aunt?" Lady Caroline asked.

"I would be honored." But he held back. "Before I do, I wonder if you might wish to take a turn in the garden. Lady Plain de Ville is famous for her . . . ," he trailed off.

Blast it all! He didn't know what the lady had in her garden. There might be an unusual fountain or some exotic plant, but he could hardly say such in case there wasn't any.

To his relief, Lady Caroline finished his thought. "Shrubberies," she offered, tilting her head mischievously.

"Yes, exactly."

"Lord Diamond, let me be clear. Normally, without a chaperone, I would not go beyond the boundaries of the ballroom with any man. But I shall go outside with you for one simple reason. I fear this may be a singular opportunity for us to speak privately. My mother will surely catch wind of our dance, and I believe I shall not be allowed to have another."

She was a reasonable female, which he appreciated. Yet he could not credit this was their one chance to be alone. He already liked her more than any woman he'd ever met. It was premature, irrational, and lunatic, but it was the bald truth.

"I understand," he told her, "although I cannot say I am happy to hear it. It seems unfair to set limitations upon us because of anything that occurred years ago."

"And that is why I will venture outside with you."

With a hand on the small of her back, he propelled her from the ballroom once again, toward the refreshment salon across the hall. Yet instead of entering with other revelers, they turned and walked swiftly along the hallway to the back staircase. In a flash, they were downstairs at the door to the garden, which turned out to be the tiniest plot with a few rose bushes and a single tree.

They stopped short on the stone terrace. You could even smell the mews behind the garden wall. No one would believe they were out there admiring anything except each other.

To his delight, she started to laugh at the absurdity. Geoffrey squeezed her hand and stepped onto the grass.

"It's a fine hazel tree," he said, gesturing to the single stunted plant.

"I believe it's a birch," Lady Caroline said, "and not the least bit fine."

"Let's circle it and see it from the other side," he suggested, emboldened by her acquiescence.

He'd always imagined ladies to be skittish and prudish, a far cry from the flash mollishers he visited at the best bawdy houses. Years earlier, he'd briefly escorted a lady whom he met through her brother, a fellow university student. A marquess's daughter, she had pursed her lips at everything Geoffrey said, yet still, he'd persevered for two weeks.

Unbelievably, without so much as a kiss, she had demanded a declaration of intent if not of actual love. At the tender age of twenty-one, he had not been remotely ready.

Seeing no point in forming an attachment to a female in whom he had no interest marrying, he'd gradually started a regular routine of engaging the excellent services of high fliers, usually keeping one of the experienced, polished whores for as long as six months.

When the time was ripe for taking a wife, Geoffrey had always planned on ceasing what some might consider to be libertine ways and become a dedicated husband, as his own father purported to be—despite what Lady Chimes might think of him.

It seemed only fair and right.

They circled the tree and were on the far side where the lamps inside the house no longer shone directly upon them.

Strangely, as he looked down at her under the moonlight, he felt a little unsure. While his body urged a smoldering embrace with her crushed against him, he reached out and trailed a gloved finger down her cheek.

"I'm glad you came tonight," he said.

"As am I. I admit I was curious about you. After my mother's refusal at Lord and Lady Fenwick's ball, I asked my aunt the reason."

"I asked my mother the same thing. I had never heard anything about your family before."

Stepping closer, Geoffrey took hold of her hands.

"Regardless," he added, "I appreciate how you didn't let any bitterness between our parents stop you from dancing with me."

She nodded before her gaze dropped to where their hands were clasped.

Not wanting to waste another moment at the wondrous opportunity to be alone with her, Geoffrey slowly drew Lady Caroline closer, his heart thumping at the notion of kissing the most gorgeous woman he'd ever seen.

He knew they should spend time talking frankly, but what if she was never again allowed to be anywhere near him? This could be his only chance, and a single kiss might prove them entirely unsuited. With that knowledge, he could put thoughts of this flame-haired lady aside.

Briefly wondering if he should ask permission to kiss her, or if that would mark him as a noodle-head, he heard himself say, "May I?"

Yet by then, it was too late. He was already lowering his mouth to hers. In the next second, he kissed her, and a tendril of passion unfurled inside him at her taste, blossoming into white-hot desire. They'd sipped the same punch, yet her mouth had the additional flavor of orange blossom and lavender flowers. He could both smell the delectable scents and experience them upon his tongue.

Releasing her hands, he slid his arms around her waist, enjoying her surprised gasp. With her lips parted, Geoffrey gently slid his tongue between them. To his joy, he felt her melt against him, with her hands suddenly behind his neck, hanging on.

When he stroked her tongue with his, she froze before tentatively echoing the movement. Tilting his head, he deepened the kiss, sucking her lower lip into his mouth.

Kissing Lady Caroline in the dark garden was the single most sensual, tantalizing thing he'd ever done, despite having tupped his share of light-skirts.

Hearing her small sigh of pleasure, for a moment of complete insanity, he considered going farther into the darkness, a mere few yards toward the brick wall. There, if she were willing, he could at least touch her skin.

Just the thought inflamed him, and he nibbled a hot trail down her neck, making her arch away and give him access to the curving upper swell of her breasts with a searing open-mouthed kiss.

"Dear God!"

CHAPTER FOUR

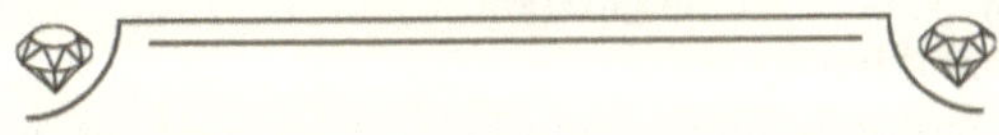

Aunt Cordelia's shocked voice was like a splash of frigid water. Lord Diamond released her so quickly, Caroline stumbled forward until he put his hands out to steady her.

At the same time, she opened her eyes as lamplight destroyed the sanctuary of their dimly lit embrace.

"You are in dreadful trouble," her aunt said. And then she added, "And so am I."

It was true. Caroline's mother would smite them both with her wrath. And who could tell what her father might do if he caught wind of it?

Next to Aunt Cordelia was their evening's hostess.

"Most unacceptable," said Lady Plain de Ville. "Shocking, in fact."

"Hardly shocking," Lord Diamond said. "It was merely a kiss."

Caroline wished he hadn't said anything. The lady's eyes widened.

"Not *merely* a kiss," pronounced their outraged hostess. "Your mouth was *not* upon her lips when we found you."

For a moment, Caroline didn't know what Lady Plain de Ville meant. Within seconds of Geoffrey touching her, she'd known nothing but excited, sizzling sensations. Her other more discerning faculties had all but shut down. And then she recalled his lips on the curve of her breast.

Looking at him, he appeared unrepentant, and she wished he wore an expression of chagrin at the very least.

Caroline decided to plead for them both. "I beg of you, my lady, not to think badly of us. We are two people who are not pledged to others. We were causing no one any harm, simply sharing a kiss, albeit perhaps a little something more than a chaste one," she added, glancing at Lord Diamond, "and therefore undoubtedly ill-advised."

Perhaps he didn't understand the dire circumstances. He made a sound of exasperation before addressing their hostess and her aunt.

"We are *not* children, and I, for one, find this snooping and spying to be beyond the pale."

Caroline wanted to clamp her hand over his mouth, but stood staring, aghast, as did her aunt and their hostess.

"We are trying to decide whether we have enough interest in one another to bother beginning a courtship," he continued. "Or at least that's what I was doing. What about you, Lady Caroline?"

Is that why they kissed? She already had quite an emphatic interest in the man, or she wouldn't have gone outside with him, but all she did was nod in agreement.

"Thus, you see, ladies, now that Lady Caroline and I have come to an understanding, we can face the rest of the obstacles of which we've been told there are at least four."

Caroline thought he summed it up well. Four parents, all determined to keep them apart.

"Aunt Cordelia, Lord Diamond and I merely wanted . . . that is, oh, please don't tell Mother and Father."

Her aunt fixed her with a stare that reminded her too much of her mother's, making Caroline shiver. But it was Lady Plain de Ville who brought it all to an end.

"I do not approve of my party, nor my garden, being used for such behavior. However, we shall say no more about it since we caught you before anything too egregious occurred."

"Then you will say nothing?" Aunt Cordelia asked.

"I don't want anyone to know of such reprehensible behavior, either. My home is *not* Vauxhall!" With that, the older lady turned heel and walked away, taking the oil lamp with her.

Lord Diamond gestured for her and Aunt Cordelia to go ahead of him, which they did.

"What now?" Caroline whispered to her aunt.

"I suppose I get to keep my head upon its shoulders," she jested. "As for you two, heaven help you if you decide to continue in this folly."

"I can hear you," Lord Diamond said, sounding annoyed. "Why is this folly?"

"While I am a sappy fool who allowed you to meet," her aunt snapped at him, "Lady Caroline's parents will not look kindly on any association. I had half-hoped my niece would find you lacking and speak no more of you. But mark me, Lord and Lady Chimes will not give their blessing and certainly not my niece's dowry to a Diamond."

Silence met those daunting words. By then, they were back inside and heading upstairs to the ballroom. Lady Plain de Ville had disappeared from view.

"Maybe Lord Diamond doesn't want an association," Caroline began.

"I believe I do," he muttered, and she almost laughed with relief for, more than anything, she wanted to get to know him better. When she stopped in her tracks at the top of the staircase, Lord Diamond ran into the back of her.

"*Ooph,*" he said. "I nearly tumbled back down to my death."

"That might have been easier on you," her aunt quipped.

Caroline ignored them both. "I merely wanted to ask if we would be allowed to dance again tonight."

Aunt Cordelia sighed. "Yes, you two can have another dance, but I shall have my eyes upon you both, and if I'm lucky, a glass of rum punch in my hand."

CAROLINE WONDERED HOW she could win either of her parents over to her side. Dancing twice with Geoffrey Diamond had been heavenly, despite Lady Plain de Ville's disapproving stare for the rest of the evening.

Moreover, every other partner that night was inconsequential in comparison, and all she could do was hope this wouldn't be the last time she was in Lord Diamond's arms.

In the carriage, her aunt was not hopeful.

"While I believe our hostess will not mention seeing you two together, the fact that you were both at this ball will most likely reach your mother's ears. You could pretend you never even saw Diamond, I suppose, but that won't get you any closer to your goal. That is, if you truly wish to have that plummy young man court you in earnest."

"I believe I do," Caroline said, echoing Lord Diamond's earlier statement. She decided to tell her parents the following day. If she was honest with them, surely they would want her happiness as they always had before.

As circumstances happened, she didn't catch them together until dinner.

"Sit," her father said as soon as she entered the dining room.

"That was my intention." Caroline glanced at the two of them. Her mother's lips were set in a straight line, and her father was drumming upon the table as if he'd been kept waiting. Unmistakable tension shrouded the room.

Her usual place on one side, halfway between them, felt like a trap, and she fervently wished one or both of her brothers were at home to offer a diversion or at least bolster her spirits.

"I hope you are both well," she started, then hurried on. "I have something to tell you."

"If it is about Diamond, we already know," her father said.

Her gaze flew to his and then back to her mother.

"From Lady Plain de Ville?" Caroline asked. If that was the case, then they knew about the kiss. *That glorious, breathtaking, soul-shattering kiss!*

"The newspaper had a paragraph about the party," her father continued, "mostly because the Diamond heir was in attendance. Word has it he's looking for a wife."

"I see." Caroline quickly decided to change tactics and let them draw any information out of her.

"Did you dance with him?" her mother asked, her tone soft, which was more cause for alarm.

She had to tell her. After all, they'd been seen dancing, and it was nothing to be ashamed of.

"Yes," she said.

Her father's hand slammed upon the tablecloth, making her jump. Her mother flinched slightly as well. But the next harsh words came from her end of the table.

"I believe I told you not to. Do you have no recollection of my refusal to allow him to be introduced?"

"Yes," Caroline said again. "But—"

"But you thought you knew better," her father ground out.

"We merely danced."

"There is no 'merely' with a Diamond," Lord Chimes said. "They want and they take."

Her mother glanced at him, her eyes widening. Caroline wondered if his words hurt her. *Did her father wish the earl hadn't taken the woman who might have become his Lady Chimes?*

"That is nothing to do with me," Caroline insisted, using all the strength of her twenty years to stand up for herself. "I enjoyed dancing with Lord Diamond and intended to tell you tonight that we had done so. Also, I would like to see him again."

Her father nearly slammed the table again. Stopping himself by fisting his hand, he ran the other over his forehead and gestured for wine from the silent footman who watched the entire scene from his place by the wall.

"Handle your daughter," Lord Chimes said to Caroline's mother without looking at either one of them.

"*Handle me?*" Caroline exclaimed. This was so unlike her normally loving and generous parents, she could almost believe she had walked into the wrong dining room. True, her father was strict with his sons, and her mother had a strong personality, but neither had ever directed any dissatisfaction toward her.

"I ask you to recall I have two decades behind me. I have met a man who interests me enough that I wish to know him better. I am not doing anything outrageous, like trying to run away with a street-sweeper. He is an earl's only son, and I have heard nothing bad about him. Indeed, I had heard nothing about him at all before the Fenwicks' ball. Moreover, he will be an earl someday."

No point in saying Diamond had alluring eyes, a wicked grin, and solid muscles she had felt for herself.

"There are other eligible men who are not street-sweepers, as you said so dramatically," her mother pointed out. "Last week, you didn't know of his existence. Next week, you can just as easily forget about him, too."

"I don't wish to forget about him. I want to—" she broke off, seeing her father start to seethe, his jaw clenching as he gritted his teeth.

"Sometimes, you don't get what you want," he said after a moment.

Again, seeing her mother's wounded expression, Caroline thought his choice of words was terribly poor. He might be speaking of the current Lady Diamond, for all she knew.

"And this is one of those times," her father continued. "You will *not* dance with him again. If you see him at a ball or a party, you will *not* speak to him, nor allow him to speak with you. Your mother will accompany you at all times to ensure that is the case."

"But I—"

"That is the end of it," Lord Chimes said. "Did I forget anything?" he asked his wife.

"No," Lady Chimes said softly. "I think you said it all."

CHAPTER FIVE

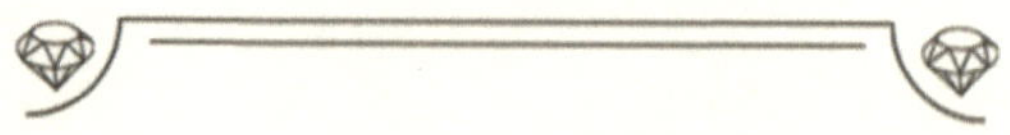

Geoffrey was determined to see Lady Caroline again. And not only to see her but to speak with her.

"It's not a case of wanting what I cannot have," he told his close friend, Jasper Trent, who thought himself clever with women. They sat at a table in White's dining room having finished a good meal. "I wanted her *before* I knew I couldn't have her."

"Then it's *Romeo and Juliet* all over again," Jasper said, sipping brandy. "You and the Chimes are the Capulets and the Montagues. Given that fact, we don't want to end with so much poisoning and death now, do we?"

Geoffrey rolled his eyes. "We shall not."

"What about her brothers?"

"What about them?"

"What if they come after you?" Jasper asked.

Geoffrey smiled wryly. "They'll have to stand in line behind their father and mother and my own father and mother first."

That tickled Jasper to no end, and he laughed at Geoffrey's expense. After a minute, however, he spoke again.

"Maybe you had best throw them off the scent."

"What do you mean?" Geoffrey asked, then drained his brandy, gesturing to the server for another.

"Escort some other young lady about Town. In fact, dance with everyone *except* Lady Caroline, don't even try to speak with her. Laugh and chat with the other females instead so your parents and hers suspect nothing of your heart."

"You dolt! That will make me look like a rake, especially to Lady Caroline. And how will that help me get closer to her?"

"I may be a dolt," Jasper said, "but I am a willing one who would carry your messages to her in your stead."

Geoffrey gaped at him. "You really do think I am Romeo come to life. That makes you Juliet's nurse, by the way, as she was the one who carried all the messages." He saw his friend smile again. "And you are liable to get me poisoned or stabbed after all."

Besides, Geoffrey didn't want to play games and pretend to care for other ladies. *Why bring more people into it?* He wanted to be frank. On the other hand, he could use Jasper's help in communicating with Lady Caroline if necessary.

As it turned out, at the next assembly in a grand house on St. James's Square, Lady Caroline was there with her indomitable mother. The woman's head appeared to be upon a swivel, and she didn't let her daughter out of her sight.

And thus, he needed Jasper after all.

"Dance with Lady Caroline," Geoffrey instructed from a position behind a column. "And please tell her I'll be waiting in the vestibule, next to the vase of flowers."

Jasper, who had made sure to gain an introduction to Caroline early during the evening, saluted rudely. "As you wish, sire."

After watching his friend take the coppery-haired Caroline as his partner, Geoffrey left the room just before the dancing ended. He waited for half an hour, but she never appeared. Eventually, forced to give up, he returned to the main hall and spotted her dancing with another gentleman, Lord Mangue.

Jasper intercepted him. "Your Juliet was willing, but there was no way for her to leave the room without her dear mother at her side."

"Then we shall have to find another way. Will you dance with her again later in the evening?"

Jasper grinned. "People will start to link *my* name with Lady Caroline's."

"I shall risk it," Geoffrey said. "Find out if she goes anywhere without her mother. With another chaperone or, better yet, with her aunt. If there is such a place, find out the time and I shall go there, too."

IT COULDN'T HAVE WORKED out better. Geoffrey met Lady Caroline at Hatchards bookshop on Piccadilly with her maid two days later. Jasper told him Lady Chimes considered it to be, in Caroline's words, "a dull outing." And therefore, safe.

Upon entering the shop at number 187 between the bay windows, Geoffrey spied Lady Caroline at once by her hair. Although under a cream-colored bonnet with a yellow ribbon, enough of her glorious locks showed like a beacon. What's more, she had claimed a space in the middle of the ground floor, perhaps in order to see him easily. Dressed in a lemon-colored gown of fine cotton, with a matching short satin spencer, she was the epitome of femininity, and he would have noticed her even if she'd been in a dark corner.

Her face lit up with a smile. He nodded, seeing her maid beside her.

Now what?

Moving closer, he browsed the books on the round tables, not actually seeing anything, too aware of her nearness.

"Keep an eye on these books," he heard her say to her maid when he was a mere few yards away. "I am going to see if they have the latest Waverly novel."

"Yes, miss."

Geoffrey waited a few moments, moving toward the bookshelves that lined the walls, keeping his back to the maid. He picked out a thick volume, inspected it, and returned it before starting to hum quietly.

Sauntering along in the direction Lady Caroline had gone, he increased his pace as soon as he was out of the maid's view.

"Here," Lady Caroline said when he nearly passed her hiding place, squeezed between two bookcases.

Grasping her hand, he pulled her along behind him farther into the back of the shop.

"That was a good ruse," he commended, "gathering up so many books your maid would have to stay put."

"It wasn't a ruse," she said. "I really shall buy them or at least some of them, with my allowance, and the Waverly novel *St. Ronan's Well*, too, if I find it."

He was impressed.

"Besides," she said, "if I went home empty-handed, that would be suspicious indeed."

"You are a clever lady," he praised.

And they reached the last of the public area at the back of the shop.

"I suppose this will have to do. Perhaps next time, we can meet upstairs."

"Next time?" she murmured softly.

He sighed. "I know this is hardly ideal, but unless your aunt accompanies you to another ball—"

"She will not. My mother won't allow her to be my chaperone again."

"I see." Geoffrey couldn't imagine how they would begin any kind of meaningful association if they could only meet for a few minutes in a dusty bookstore.

"There is always Gretna Green," he said.

Lady Caroline visibly startled.

"Merely a jest," he assured her, although if he did fall in love and there was no other way, he was not entirely opposed to a Scottish border wedding.

They remained silent a moment. He didn't find it the least bit awkward, happy simply to be in her presence.

"My friend, Lord Trent, doesn't mind carrying messages between us," he said.

"That's kind of him. And he is a good dancer." Suddenly, she sighed. "This is ridiculous."

He flinched. *Was she ready to give up?*

"What can my parents do if you simply come claim me for a dance at the next ball?"

Relieved to learn not only wasn't she giving up, Lady Caroline was ready to stand up to her parents, he drew her into his arms. Instantly, a sizzling heat raced through him. His attraction to her was like nothing he'd ever experienced.

Without asking or waiting, he lowered his head and kissed her. At once, she melted against him. Having never swived with a woman he was in love with, he could easily imagine how good it would be with a beloved wife. One could take years to explore the other's needs and desires. That might be life's best adventure of all.

With her hands grasping his arms, he tilted his head and kissed her as thoroughly as he could against shelves of books that threatened to tumble down upon them. Their tongues danced briefly, and she sighed into his mouth, making his loins take distinct notice.

Wanting to plunge his hands into her hair and disturb the pins and her adorable yellow bonnet, instead Geoffrey took care not to leave her in the slightest disarray.

"My lady," came her maid's voice, and they broke apart.

Dammit all! he swore silently. "We hardly had a minute, it seems. Can you be at Vauxhall tomorrow night?"

Her eyes were a little glazed, and he was pleased to have caused her distracted expression.

"I believe so," she said. "I've been once before, and Mother said we could return. If the weather is fine, she will allow it."

"If you come, Lord Trent will find you between the Turkish Tent and where the orchestra plays. He shall tell you where I am."

"It's pointless," she began. "Wherever I go, my mother will, too."

"Don't you have a friend you can meet by chance and walk with? Maybe if Trent escorts you to the Rotunda, I can run into you."

"Maybe," she said, sounding forlorn but tugging on her spencer to make sure she was in good order.

"Tell me why you taste of orange and lavender," he asked.

"Lip balm," she said.

"You taste delicious."

That brought a smile back to her face. "What's your favorite color?" she asked in return.

"My lady?" came the maid again.

"Why?" he asked.

"I simply want to learn more about you. If I come away with a little nugget of information after each meeting, eventually, I'll know you."

"At this rate, I will need a cane before you get through my likes and dislikes."

"I must go," she said. "Tell me your answer."

Without hesitation, he said, "Your hair. That is my favorite color."

Her cheeks pinkened, and she turned to leave.

"And yours?" he asked quietly.

She glanced back at him. "Blue," she said, gesturing at her own gown. "Like your eyes."

And then she was gone.

CHAPTER SIX

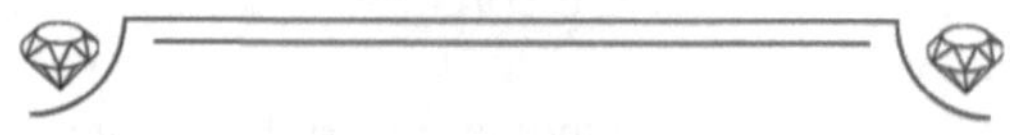

Vauxhall Pleasure Gardens were as Caroline remembered them—bustling, loud, and thrilling. And this time, she knew Geoffrey Diamond was awaiting her.

Unfortunately, her mother had taken to the idea so readily because both she and Caroline's father would enjoy the evening. Also, Lord Mangue would be there. Lady Chimes had fixed herself upon the idea that if only Caroline spent more time with the viscount, then she would find herself developing a *tendre* in no time at all.

Caroline ignored the knowledge that he would be thrown in her path that night. At the very least, if she gave Lord Mangue a modicum of attention, it would keep her mother from watching her too closely. Moreover, her best friend, Daphne, had responded to an eager request for her presence, agreeing to come since her husband was away overseeing their country estate.

Daphne, whom Caroline had known in Bath, had fallen wildly in love, married young, and she and Lord Hollidge already had a dear little boy. Caroline could only hope for similar happiness.

Thus, she and her parents along with Daphne, whom they had collected at her home, stepped off the ferry boat that carried them swiftly from Westminster to the south bank of the Thames. After climbing the Vauxhall steps, as they'd been dubbed a century earlier, the four of them entered through the proprietor's house. Out the back door, they spilled into the wondrous acreage known as the Vauxhall Pleasure Gardens.

Immediately, the excitement of the spectacle took hold of Caroline. It was impossible not to feel a thrill when taking in the long walks, dining pavilions, groves and grottoes, colonnades and music, and twenty thousand oil lamps hanging from every branch and structure. Add to that the myriad entertainment and crowds of revelers, and it was impossible for one's heart not to pound a little more quickly.

After they were assigned one of the supper boxes on the left side of the garden by the Chinese Temples, she and Daphne were ready either to stroll toward the orchestra or to tour the grounds with her parents.

As if it hadn't been planned by Lady Chimes, Lord Mangue arrived, expressing delight upon seeing them.

"Well met," he said all around.

Thwarting his hope to monopolize her company, however, Lord Trent also appeared. Thus, after a few minutes of prattle with her parents, the four single people went to the area where couples danced by the so-called Gothic Orchestra, a two-story structure housing the musicians on the open-air second floor.

Lord Mangue took her in his arms without asking.

As soon as the dance ended, Lord Trent smoothly suggested he and Mangue switch partners.

"You did that expertly," Caroline told him.

"My dance steps?" Lord Trent asked innocently.

"You know what I mean," she said. Then feeling like an English spy in Paris or a Bow Street detective, she asked, "Where is Lord Diamond?"

"Down the Grand South Walk near the third Triumphal Arch," Lord Trent responded. "You know, he is a good chap. It's a pity about your parents and his."

"A pity, indeed," she agreed.

A few minutes later, when the dance ended and the orchestra took a break, Lord Trent returned her to her parents' table. Daphne and Lord Mangue arrived a moment later.

"May I escort these two lovely ladies down the Grand South Walk?" Lord Trent asked. "We'll go down one side and back up the other. As a married lady and mother, Lady Hollidge must be considered a suitable chaperone."

"As long as you don't go as far as the Firework Tower," Lord Chimes warned. "I don't want these girls anywhere near the Dark Walk."

"We shall turn on the path by the third arch," Lord Trent promised.

Caroline thought Geoffrey's plan was going exceedingly well, but Lord Mangue was not to be left out.

"Capital idea," he said, earning Caroline's mother's nod of approval. "Lord Trent and I shall keep them safe and enjoy the gardens at the same time."

Caroline's heart sank. *How would she get away from him?*

The four of them departed the Grove to promenade down the Grand South Walk toward the less busy sections of the Pleasure Gardens.

Simply knowing Lord Diamond was nearby had Caroline tingling with excitement. As they approached the third Triumphal Arch where Lord Trent had indicated Geoffrey would be, the hair on the back of her neck rose, imagining him watching from the darkness. They turned as promised to cross the width of the gardens.

A moment later, Lord Diamond sauntered toward them, hailing his friend Lord Trent and also greeting Lord Mangue.

"Do you know Lady Caroline and Lady Hollidge?" Lord Trent asked his friend, sounding sincere.

"I have had the pleasure of making Lady Caroline's acquaintance," Lord Diamond acknowledged, taking her hand and bowing over it, giving her knuckles a gentle squeeze before he released her.

"And while I have met Lord Hollidge at my club, I have not yet been introduced to his lovely wife. Good evening, Lady Hollidge." He turned his full attention upon Daphne, taking her hand and bowing over it.

Caroline almost wished Daphne were single at that moment, for then Lord Diamond could feign interest in her. If he were linked with Daphne in the public's perception, then they could be near one another more easily.

"Even though it is an odd number, my lord, if you are alone, why don't you join our happy group," Caroline offered.

"How gracious of you," Lord Diamond said.

Soon the five of them were watching the rope-dancing theatre. If only Lord Mangue wasn't there, Caroline could speak freely in front of their respective friends. Yet despite wracking her brain, she could think of no way to put the man off.

"Are you here escorting your sister?" Lord Diamond suddenly asked Lord Mangue.

"No, why do you ask?"

Lord Diamond made a great show of appearing mortified. "I should have said nothing. I apologize."

Alarmed, Lord Mangue insisted he answer. "Tell me, Diamond."

"I would swear I saw her earlier when I arrived. She has brown hair and a single mole on her cheek, does she not?"

"She does, but my family made no mention of her coming here tonight, nor can I imagine whom she was with."

Lord Diamond gave a grimacing smile. "No matter, then. She wasn't actually with anyone. Walking along on this very path when I last saw her, and she was quite alone, so that's fine."

"Are you mad?" Lord Mangue exclaimed. "That's not fine at all. Tell me precisely where she was going."

Lord Diamond widened his eyes as if only just realizing something.

"Come to think of it, Mangue, I believe she was heading toward," he paused, looking toward the far wall at the back of Vauxhall's acreage before he whispered, "the Dark Walk."

Lord Mangue reared back as if facing a tiger.

"You probably should make sure she is well," Lord Trent advised. "Although odds are she was meeting a friend and isn't alone any longer."

"What are you saying?" Lord Mangue demanded.

"I only mean the way Lady Caroline might meet up with Lady Hollidge. What did you think I meant?"

"I cannot abandon Lady Caroline," Lord Mangue fretted. "I told her parents I would escort her."

"Please, my lord. You should go find her at once," Caroline said. "I have these two gentlemen and my good friend with me. I would never forgive myself if anything happened to your sister with no one at all to protect her."

"Yes, you're correct. I bid you good evening." He didn't even wait to say goodbye to the rest of them before hurrying away.

"Poor girl, I hope she is unharmed," Daphne said.

Caroline nodded, but when she caught Lord Diamond's eye, she nearly began to laugh.

Lord Trent shook his head. "Remarkable that you could see a girl's mole in this dusky light."

"Amazing, isn't it?" Lord Diamond said. "I do hope it was the correct lady."

Just then, the bell announced the start of the mysterious Cascade. And they moved toward it as did many other of the gardens' visitors. Somehow, Caroline found Lord Diamond directly beside her.

"Are you interested in this?" he asked.

"It is amusing, don't you think?" When she'd seen the mock waterfall and fake mechanized carriage crossing the bridge the first time, she had never seen anything like it before or since.

"I find *you* far more amusing and interesting," Lord Diamond said. "Shall we take a stroll?"

Caroline tensed. This was not the safety of Lady Plain de Ville's tiny plot of garden. This was Vauxhall where reputations were ruined on a nightly basis.

"Just to talk," he added.

Caroline hesitated. She barely knew him, but what she did know, she liked. And again, this might be one of the few, precious moments they could spend in one another's company.

She nodded.

"Lady Caroline and I are going to take a walk. We shall return here shortly."

"This show lasts about a quarter of an hour," Lord Trent reminded them.

Lord Diamond nodded. "I shall have her back here and in time for you to escort her to her parents."

"Understood," Lord Trent said.

Daphne was watching with her mouth in the shape of an O, and Caroline knew she would have to explain it all to her later.

WHEN GEOFFREY GOT LADY Caroline alone in Vauxhall, he surprised himself. The first thing he wanted to do was talk with her, not kiss her, despite wanting very much to do that as well.

"I want to know everything about you," he confessed, drawing her arm through his and continuing to move along the path, so they didn't appear scandalous. "Do you enjoy riding?"

"Very much."

"And boating?" he prompted.

"Do you mean rowing or sailing?" she asked.

"Either. Both, I suppose."

"I have sailed across the Channel to France, but I would very much enjoy an outing in a rowboat."

"I would enjoy rowing you wherever you wish. As long as it's upon water."

She laughed, a beautiful warm sound.

"What is your favorite season?" he continued.

"Spring. It brings such promise for the year, as well as flowers."

"A good answer," he said.

"And you, my lord?"

"I believe I like summer best when that spring promise has been fulfilled with sunshine and warmer weather," he said. "Is there a food you most favor?"

"I like this game," she said. "No gentleman has ever asked my opinion on even the most mundane things."

"I honestly don't think I've ever asked another female about her likes, so I cannot speak too ill of my fellow sex in that regard. Only when a man is truly taken with a woman does he care to know more."

He felt her shiver. "Are you cold?"

"No, not in the least. In answer to your previous question, I enjoy roasted chicken, and I adore sponge cake with thick, warm custard. And now, it is my turn to ask," she said. "What is your favorite taste?"

His loins tightened at once, and the answer came easily. "You, my lady."

Her gasp was nearly silent. Then she laughed. "Be serious."

"I am. When I kissed you the first time, I thought you tasted better than anything else in the world."

Lady Caroline said nothing for a moment, then spoke. "It was simply the orange blossom and lavender beeswax balm."

"Maybe at first, but only when mixed with the essence of you. I kissed your skin, too, you may recall. I thought all of you to be exquisite."

She shook her head and touched her gloved palm to her face, dropping it quickly in case she was seen.

"You speak like a lover," she said.

"Or like a man falling in love."

CHAPTER SEVEN

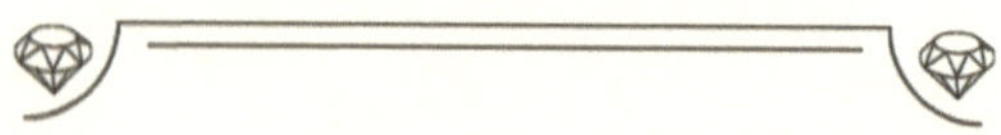

Geoffrey said the words spontaneously, not to intrigue or ensnare her. Yet as soon as they were out of his mouth, he considered their absolute truth. He would not confess to already loving her, yet his heart might say differently.

Lady Caroline stopped and turned to face him, even as others walked around them along the path.

"I know precisely what you mean. Strange as it may sound, I feel attracted to you beyond reason, beyond the shallow knowledge I have of you, and certainly beyond the little amount of time we have shared."

Hearing her confession, he nearly drew her close, then recalled where they were.

"I would like to kiss you again," he said frankly, "but I think it would be better to act honorably if we have any chance of winning over your parents."

"What about yours?" she asked.

He shrugged. "My parents do not control whom I marry, nor do I live with them. Thus, it is yours we must succeed in placating."

She sighed. "I believe you are correct. Shall we return to our friends?"

Thus, after being alone with a woman at Vauxhall, he returned her to Trent and Lady Hollidge without having kissed her. *It was almost unnatural!*

Ignoring Jasper's knowing look—*the devil take him!*—Geoffrey had to leave Lady Caroline in his safe hands and watch the three walk away. It was irksome and as she'd once said, it was plainly ridiculous. They were being penalized for something that had occurred before either of them was born.

It was time to speak with his father.

A short while later, Geoffrey entered his parents' house, hoping they were at home. For all he knew, he'd just left them behind in Vauxhall. His luck held. Not only were they there, they were together, both of them in the upstairs salon, wearing slippers and dressing gowns, sipping brandy and reading.

Lord and Lady Diamond were the picture of domesticity, which tickled him considering his parents' reputations as being a little wild when they were younger.

After kissing his mother's cheek and accepting his father's offer of French brandy, Geoffrey suddenly wasn't sure if he ought to speak privately with the earl. If there was something unsavory in his father's past of which his mother was unaware, he would become as tight-lipped as a clam.

Deciding to risk it, Geoffrey flopped down in a chair and poured from the decanter on the table beside him.

"I saw Lady Caroline Chimes tonight at Vauxhall."

Both his parents lowered their books.

"That was unwise," remarked his father, James Diamond, "but probably a delightful experience, nonetheless."

His mother, on the other hand, narrowed her eyes. "Not if she was with her parents. In which case, I'm sure you had a ghastly time of it."

"I didn't meet with Lord and Lady Chimes. In case you've forgotten, I am not allowed," Geoffrey said, hoping all his frustration was in his voice. "Because of the two of you."

His father started to laugh until his mother jabbed him in the ribs with her elbow.

"Why must you be so intent upon this particular girl?" she asked. "There are marriageable young ladies all over London."

"What do you mean *intent* on her?" his father asked. "What have I missed?"

"Geoffrey spotted Lady Caroline at the Fenwicks' ball. Lady Chimes gave him a public dressing down and refused an introduction."

His father looked unimpressed. "And now you're going out of your way to try to meet your elusive, impossible quarry, is that it? Is she a copper-haired beauty like her mother or a sandy-brown toad like her father?"

Geoffrey gripped his glass tighter, irritated by the earl for making light of the situation.

"I have succeeded in gaining an introduction to Lady Caroline," he said, "at Lady Plain de Ville's home. And I have come to admire her greatly, but Lord and Lady Chimes have forbidden us to keep company, not even to dance."

"You have come to admire her," her mother echoed. "I take it you've had more than a single introduction."

That was not their business. Geoffrey shrugged, making his father laugh again.

"What do you want us to do? Grant our blessing?" Lord Diamond gestured to Geoffrey to hand him the decanter so he could refill his glass.

"As if we would do that," his mother said. "Blessing, indeed!"

"Why?" Geoffrey snapped.

"That mushroom," she began, but he interrupted her.

"Why do you call Lady Chimes such a thing?"

"Because she sprung up out of nowhere and landed in the titled class with nothing more than a baronet for a father and no dowry to speak of, or so I've heard."

The earl crossed his arms and said nothing.

"Come along, Father. Surely you have an opinion."

"On Lady Chimes? No, not really. I don't know her. I saw her years ago. She's beautiful though, with that fiery hair I mentioned."

"When?" Lady Diamond demanded. "When did you see her?"

Geoffrey's father sighed. "It was probably at that ball when you and I arrived together as a couple for the first time. I thought Chimes was going to fall upon his sword. Instead, suddenly, he was dancing with her, looking pleased as Mr. Punch."

"You noticed her?" Lady Diamond asked.

"Only because of her hair, my love. Obviously, she can't hold a candle to you. If she could, then I would be with her instead."

He laughed hard at that, but by her scowl, Geoffrey's mother didn't think her husband the least bit amusing.

"I'm only teasing," the earl reminded his wife, draping his arm along the back of the sofa and around her slender shoulders. "Remember, once I saw you, I had to have you, despite how you were ill-advisedly keeping company with Chimes."

"Hardly that," she grumbled. "He and I had barely enjoyed a few dances."

"That's not how I recall it," Lord Diamond said, his tone growing serious for the first time. "I believe there was riding and a dinner party or two, as well."

"Excuse me, dear parents, but while this stroll through your memories is as fascinating as waiting for bread to rise—"

"When have you ever done that?" his mother demanded.

"Never," Geoffrey quipped. "Because it would be boring and tedious and not worth my time, precisely like this entire discussion. All I want to know is whether either of you or both of you perpetrated some wrong upon the Chimes and if I can do anything to fix it."

His parents looked at one another and then back at him.

"We have always acted with the utmost decorum," his mother said, "except for what I told you before."

"What did you tell him?" Lord Diamond asked.

"Just that you stole me from Lord Chimes and also beat him in a wager at your club."

His father nearly spat out his brandy, which expensive as it was would have been a damn shame.

"How did you know about that?"

His mother smiled with satisfaction. "We wives have our ways of knowing what goes on at those gentlemen's clubs."

The next thing Geoffrey knew, his feisty parents were arguing loudly about "interfering, nosy-poke harpies" and "depraved, pompous bucks."

Sighing, Geoffrey downed his brandy and rose to his feet. They didn't even notice. In any case, he doubted they would ever be the least bit helpful.

AFTER VAUXHALL, CAROLINE endured a series of frustrating experiences. Inside the new National Gallery, at number 100 Pall Mall, she was with her mother when she spied Geoffrey, as Caroline now dared to think of him. He saw her nearly at the same moment. They both pretended to look at the works by Raphael and Hogarth while surreptitiously sneaking glances at one another.

Finally, Caroline's mother caught sight of him, and they left without her getting to exchange more than a smile with him.

Then there was the night at the theatre when she and her parents had been in the same audience as the King and Queen of the Sandwich Islands. Despite the impressive six-foot king and his exotic queen, she'd noticed Geoffrey in his family's private box and soon had his attention. When the theater was darkened and the performance began, she still stared in his direction. And when the lamps were lit once more, they practically had a conversation across the expanse of the theatre with smiles and nods. She even risked the smallest of waves.

Finally, they were both at the same ball, and she prepared herself for another exasperating experience. Recalling what she'd said to Geoffrey, she wondered what her parents would do if he boldly came over and led her to the dance floor.

She sighed. It would be a disaster, and she couldn't pretend otherwise. Caroline's mother was not above grabbing her daughter by the ear and forcibly removing her. It would be humiliating. And despite being twenty, she imagined her father could and would confine her to their home for the rest of the Season.

Daphne, who was also at the ball, knew her sorrowful situation but had no suggestions. When Lord Hollidge was around her, as he was that night, her best friend was so madly in love, she only half-listened. Moreover, Daphne kept her eyes upon her husband, who gazed at her in return with equal ardor.

Geoffrey stayed on the opposite side of the room until Caroline accepted a partner. Each time she did, he would quickly ask a lady to dance and thus be nearby.

Shaking her head at him, she wished he would give up. While she wasn't jealous of each and every pretty miss whom he took for a partner, she was dreadfully envious.

And then Daphne, bless her heart, with her cheeks in full bloom from having danced with her husband, announced a dinner party at her home. By the sparkle in her friend's eyes, Caroline guessed Geoffrey would be invited, too.

"I shall send out the invitations over the next couple of days," Daphne told Lady Chimes just before the ball ended. "Naturally, we will have musicians and perhaps some other entertainment."

"We shall be pleased to come," Caroline's mother agreed.

"Oh, I am sorry, my lady. My husband and I are hosting this dinner only for unmarried people. No chaperones are needed nor allowed as there will not be even one unsupervised minute."

"It's a modern notion," Lady Chimes said, "but I understand the fun of young people gathering together without their parents. I wonder if I can request any particular bachelors. My daughter is becoming fond of Lord Mangue. Isn't that right?"

"Which one is he, Mother?" Caroline asked, hoping to dissuade her from pushing him toward her despite having danced with him again that night.

"Stop teasing! You know very well he's that sturdy, solid viscount."

With the single eyebrow, Caroline added silently. In truth, she was getting used to it, like a friendly caterpillar crawling across his forehead.

"I'm sure Lady Hollidge has a guest list in mind, Mother. We cannot start inserting our own guests into her party."

"I shall certainly add Lord Mangue to my guest list," Daphne promised, doing a better job of appeasing Caroline's mother than she could do herself.

"What a generous hostess and a respectful young lady," Lady Chimes said, piercing Caroline with a look that said she wished she were more like her friend.

Caroline didn't care. She'd been given permission to go to a dinner party, and she would be there *without* her mother. If Lord Diamond agreed to go, she would be satisfied Fortuna had turned her wheel.

CHAPTER EIGHT

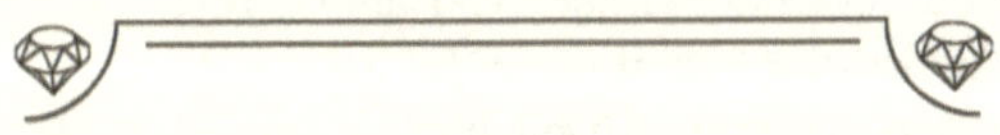

Lord and Lady Hollidge's home on Grosvenor Square, shared by Daphne, her beloved Thomas, and their young son Alexander was not far from Caroline's parents' own townhouse on Upper Brook Street, practically around the corner. Regardless, her mother had their carriage brought around from the mews, and she rode with Caroline to deposit her upon Daphne's doorstep.

"Good night, Mother. I shall see you anon." For Daphne would make sure she got home in her own carriage in the wee hours after the party.

In seven minutes, she waited excitedly in the drawing room with a glass of wine in hand, waiting for Geoffrey Diamond. Not that her friend would willfully go against the wishes of Lady Chimes. However, since Daphne could claim ignorance of any ill feelings between the Chimes and the Diamonds, she had simply included him with the other eligible men.

"But why did you actually invite Lord Mangue?" Caroline asked, when she saw him enter.

"When your mother finds out Lord Diamond is here, she won't think I did it on purpose if her favorite is also attending," Daphne explained.

Caroline supposed her friend was correct, but with Lord Mangue peering at her from under his brow, she wondered how she would be able to speak freely with Geoffrey.

"The place cards on the table will undoubtedly please you," Daphne told her with a wink before she went to greet other guests.

Before Lord Mangue could move into the vacated space, Geoffrey appeared in the doorway. Caroline waved him over, unable to contain her enthusiasm.

"Good evening, Lady Caroline. You are looking especially breathtaking tonight."

She liked the term he used, having dressed in her favorite shade of green, hoping to please him.

"You are no more handsome than usual," she returned. Lowering her voice, she added, "And yet you are still the most attractive man here."

It hardly seemed possible that every other gentleman in the room paled in comparison, but they did. She especially adored the rich raven-color of his hair and how his blue eyes contrasted with his dark lashes.

Suddenly, Lord Mangue was at her elbow. "Good evening, Lady Caroline."

"Good evening, my lord. I didn't know you were acquainted with the Hollidges."

She wished Daphne hadn't thought it necessary to be cautious in this instance and to please Caroline's mother.

"I am not, except for meeting Lady Hollidge at Vauxhall. Apparently, one of the young ladies here tonight asked for me particularly to be invited. I wonder whom it could be," Lord Mangue mused with a cock of his head.

Her stomach twinged. She hoped Geoffrey didn't think she'd had anything to do with it. All she could do was nod politely.

Then Lord Mangue turned to Geoffrey, and his greeting was less pleasant. "It seems you keep cropping up wherever Lady Caroline and I happen to be."

"I don't think that's the case," Geoffrey answered lightly. "Merely a happy circumstance."

"*Happy?*" Lord Mangue frowned, causing his single eyebrow to crease in the center. "Hardly. And do you know what, Diamond?"

"No," Geoffrey said, not asking the question Lord Mangue wished him to.

"Well, I'll tell you. My sister was most definitely *not* at Vauxhall. I meant to let you know when I saw you again, but you were always on the other side of the room at the last ball."

Geoffrey shrugged. "Better to be safe than sorry, as they say."

"Lord Diamond is correct," Caroline spoke up. "Imagine if it had been your sister, and you hadn't gone to her aid. You would never have forgiven yourself. You probably should thank Lord Diamond."

"But it wasn't Lettie! That's the point," Lord Mangue fumed. "I missed out on the rest of the evening with you."

"I kept her company," Geoffrey added wickedly, causing Lord Mangue to narrow his eyes in his direction.

Caroline wished Geoffrey wouldn't tease, nor bring attention to any time they'd spent in one another's company, especially not to Lord Mangue.

"Are you sure you even saw anyone who looked like my sister?" he demanded.

"Oh, very sure, Mangue. Mole and all."

"Lord Mangue, will you come greet the other guests?" This from Daphne, who like an angel was trying to draw him away.

"You must meet everyone," Caroline insisted when he hesitated. "You wouldn't want to insult our hosts, nor miss out on meeting whichever young lady requested your presence."

He glanced at her and a smug smile appeared. "I see. Trying to throw me off the track like a red-headed vixen. I shall make the rounds and return."

"Don't hurry," Geoffrey muttered when Lord Mangue finally walked away.

It was a brief respite from the tension between the two gentlemen. By the evening's end, though, Caroline felt as though they were engaged in a tug of war with her as the rope. She sat beside Geoffrey for dinner, which had been extremely pleasant, allowing them to discuss each course with a measure of mirth, as well as learn more of their food likes and dislikes.

However, she ended up next to Lord Mangue for the concert, with no way to change seats without causing a huge disruption.

Finally, while they were having glasses of madeira during a beautiful dramatic recitation by Daphne, whose husband accompanied her softly on his violin, Geoffrey moved toward the drawing-room door.

He didn't even have to look at her for Caroline to know he wished her to follow.

After waiting an interminable two minutes which she counted in her head, she leaned toward Lord Mangue.

"I shall be back shortly."

"I'll accompany you," he offered, starting to rise.

"No," she snapped. Then more graciously, "I am only going to the water closet."

His cheeks turned red at the mere mention of such a private task, and she hurried away. The hallway seemed deserted, and Caroline had no idea which way to go.

"*Psst,*" came a sound from farther along the dimly lit hall, and she followed it.

Near the cellar door where the kitchen was housed, there was a butler's pantry for serving the drawing room and other rooms on the main floor. Its door was ajar. As she approached, Geoffrey reached out and drew her swiftly inside.

Without preamble, his arms went around her. When he molded her body to his, heat sizzled through her.

"That was torture," he ground out before kissing her.

As he slid his tongue between her lips, she slipped her hands up and around the back of his neck, flattening her breasts against him.

In response to her acquiescence, his hand roamed down her back to cup her rounded backside, tilting her hips against his. A wicked, desperate yearning unfolded deep inside her.

"Geoffrey," she said his given name against his mouth, simply because she could.

"Yes, Caroline," he replied, and she shivered at the intimacy.

Tilting her head and going up on tiptoe, she wanted to get as close to him as she could, until she could feel his arousal pressed against her.

"I want more," she confessed.

"As do I."

She knew a little of what that meant but didn't see how anything meaningful could be accomplished in a pantry. Its cold-water sink, cupboards filled with all manner of tableware, and narrow shelves with glasses and teacups did not exactly inspire passion, despite decanters of ruby-red claret standing ready.

To her amazement, Geoffrey lifted her by the waist, turned quickly, and set her upon the marble countertop over a bank of glass-front cupboards. With her dress drawn tightly, he was unable to stand between her legs. Thus, he drew her skirts up both legs until her gown and petticoat rested atop her knees, which he gently pushed apart.

As soon as he settled between her thighs, he began to kiss her again.

Caroline had accepted all his outrageous actions with wide eyes until his mouth covered hers once more. The thrill of feeling air upon her silk stockings made her giddy, even light-headed. Sinking her hands into his hair, she opened her mouth and let their kiss deepen.

His tongue explored her mouth most thoroughly, and when she tried to do the same, he sucked upon hers, causing her toes to curl with longing.

"I'm tingling everywhere," she said quietly after he drew back, and they both were dragging in long, ragged breaths.

"As am I," he confessed, sounding hoarse. "You have bewitched me."

She giggled, too loudly, and he clamped a swift hand over her mouth.

"*Shh.*"

She nodded. She would try to rein in her happiness, but when he took his hand away, shocking words came out.

"Touch me," she asked brazenly, because she knew enough from the books she had been forbidden to read and had read anyway that if a man touched her between her legs, it would be like nothing she'd ever experienced. And that was precisely where she was throbbing.

The fingers of his right hand trailed along the path her skirts had taken, up and over her knees, across the warm flesh of her inner thigh, making her tremble.

Holding her breath until the moment he brushed against her damp and silky core, she gasped and closed her eyes.

Immediately, his lips nuzzled the exposed column of her neck while wantonly, she tilted her hips, straining to deepen his too-delicate touch.

Knowing what she wanted, Geoffrey slid a finger between her plump folds, stroking with greater vigor directly where she pulsed.

It took almost no time at all until Caroline was clinging to his shoulders while her body throbbed and tightened. And then, for a few moments, she forgot everything—that she was an earl's daughter. That she was in a butler's pantry. That she was a lady who didn't allow a man to take liberties.

Moaning loudly, she quivered, arching and tightening until a flooding release left her entirely spent.

When his hand stopped touching her, she opened her eyes and looked directly into his vivid blue gaze.

"Dear God!" she exclaimed too loudly.

"I think that came from in there," said a voice sounding unbelievably like her mother's.

Terror shot through Caroline, replacing all the ecstasy she'd experienced mere moments before. Shoving desperately at Geoffrey, who hurriedly stepped back, she frantically pushed at her skirts.

When the door opened, she was still sliding down the face of the cabinets, but at least she didn't appear to have recently had a man nestled between her legs. Regardless, her mother watched the moment her daughter's feet touched the floor, and then Lord Mangue's face appeared. There might be others in the hallway for all Caroline knew, but the room was too small to hold them.

"What is the meaning of this?" Lady Chimes demanded.

"We were just talking," Caroline said. Her voice sounded high and strained to her own ears.

"I am to blame," Geoffrey said. "Lady Caroline was walking by, and I invited her in here to chat."

"You are a dog!" Lord Mangue said.

"Is there a dog in my house?" Daphne asked from the hallway, trying to make light of it.

"Be careful what happens here," Geoffrey warned, speaking only to Lady Chimes. "Your daughter's reputation and future are at stake."

"You should have thought of that," Caroline's mother said, anger lacing every word.

"Your cheeks are frightfully flushed," Lord Mangue pointed out.

"Yes, I was feeling unwell, looking for the water closet, as I told you."

"This is *not* a water closet," her mother pointed out.

"Is everything all right?" Daphne asked, and if not for Lord Mangue, leaning against the door, she would have opened it.

"We are fine," Lady Chimes said. "My daughter didn't feel well and wandered in here by mistake. Will you clear the hallway please, Lady Hollidge, to give her some privacy? I shall take her home at once."

"I will still marry you," Lord Mangue declared.

"Marry?" repeated Caroline and Geoffrey at the same time.

"Yes, as arranged. I know this rascal was kissing you, but that is forgivable. I have kissed a few ladies. It meant nothing."

Geoffrey turned to her. "Did you know about this? That you were promised to him?"

Caroline nodded. "I knew that—"

"I don't want you speaking to my daughter. I don't want you even to look at her." Lady Chimes spoke with a tone of icy determination. "I know you did this deliberately, exactly as your father did with your mother. Is that the only way a Diamond man can get a woman to marry him? By compromising her?"

Geoffrey went tight-lipped, clenching his jaw until Caroline thought he might grind his teeth to powder.

"She's not compromised," Lord Mangue insisted.

However, Caroline kept her gaze upon Geoffrey. "Did your father risk your mother's reputation?" *If Lord Diamond had, wouldn't Geoffrey have known better than to do the same?*

"Risk it?" her mother exclaimed. "He shredded it. And yet for that, I have the Earl of Diamond to thank." She turned to Geoffrey. "Otherwise, my dear Chimes might have been saddled with your debauched mother as a wife."

"If you were a man," Geoffrey said, "I would call you out for those words."

Caroline stepped between them. "If my mother speaks the truth, then there is nothing over which you could call her out."

She ignored Geoffrey's livid expression and turned to her mother.

"As I said, I don't feel well. I'm glad you came back to fetch me. Take me home, please."

"Move aside," Lady Chimes said to Lord Mangue, who was still hovering.

"Yes, my lady. Of course. I shall call upon you tomorrow." Opening the door, he stepped into the hallway. "There is no one visible."

Without another word, her mother walked out, knowing Caroline would follow. Her mantle was on the bench by the front door, thoughtfully put out by Daphne.

Lord Mangue accompanied them to their awaiting carriage and even assisted them inside.

"Thank you," her mother said frostily.

And then neither of them spoke another word for the brief journey home, except when Caroline asked, "What made you return?"

Lady Chimes shrugged. "Mother's intuition." Then she sighed and lapsed into silence again.

Caroline had behaved abominably, as had Geoffrey Diamond. She hadn't even looked back to see what became of him.

When they reached their own front hall, Lady Chimes dumped her cloak and hat on the hall stand and mounted the stairs. Following her, Caroline watched her mother's rigid, regal rear heading along the hallway.

Outside her own bedroom door, Caroline knew she ought to at least offer thanks.

"Mother, I—"

"Not another word," Lady Chimes said, then stopped without turning. "Not tonight. We shall talk in the morning. But you should count your blessings before you lay your head upon the pillow. You still have your reputation and a fiancé. You could have been left with absolutely nothing."

And then her mother continued toward her own room, entered, and slammed the door.

Caroline had faced the evening with such anticipation and delight. Now, she dreaded what the morning would bring.

CHAPTER NINE

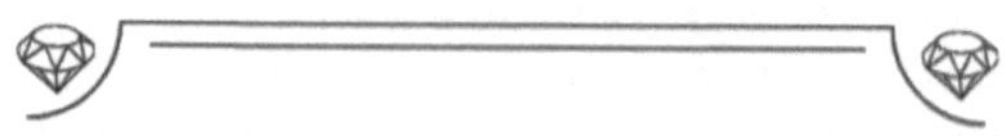

Geoffrey stormed through his house, wanting to throw something, anything. Mostly he wanted to plant a facer directly into Mangue's sappy, concerned visage. *And why didn't the man's valet trim his ridiculous single eyebrow?* Surely someone ought to tell him he looked like a monkey.

And yet Caroline had an understanding with him!

That fact, Geoffrey could simply not fathom. Her words, "Yes, I knew," continuously crashed down upon him like a wall of crumbling bricks.

How could she possibly have said yes to Mangue? At the same time, she continued to keep furtive company with him, enjoying every clandestine meeting.

For two people meant to stay apart, they'd managed to kiss many times. *And more!*

Shaking his head, he stalked through his silent townhouse, unable to sit. He'd only pleasured her in the butler's pantry because he believed they were going to figure out a way to be together. Never would he have let himself get carried away if he had truly thought she was already spoken for.

Regardless of his father's outrageous past, Geoffrey didn't go around ruining ladies! Not even ones who all but begged to be ruined.

Why would she do such a thing if she was promised to Mangue?

Unless she was being forced.

He stopped. *Of course!* She didn't want Mangue. The man was titled and had a good fortune, but that was all that recommended him. Geoffrey had jumped to conclusions, and now it would be even harder to get close to Caroline to speak to her.

Hastening to his study, he picked up a piece of cream-colored paper. Then he dropped it. He couldn't risk putting anything in writing. Without regard for the time, he donned his jacket and left for Trent's house. If he didn't find him at home, he would track him to their club.

A half hour later, he was satisfied Jasper would get a message to Caroline.

"Simply tell her to return to Hatchards tomorrow at the same time as previously."

"Ridiculous," Jasper said. "I cannot even promise to see her tomorrow. And if I do, I highly doubt she can drop everything and go to a bookseller. You had best make it the following day."

"Very well." Frustration welled in him.

"But don't expect too much," Jasper added. "After all, I may be refused entrance."

"Why would you be?" Geoffrey realized he was running his hands through his hair like a madman.

"If your lady-friend is in disgrace and has been forced to accept an offer," Jasper said, "then maybe she won't be allowed to see any other man, including me."

In disgrace! Geoffrey felt his heart sink. If she was, it was because of him. He should have been more careful. *What a clod pate!*

"Do your best," he said. "Whatever it takes to get a message to her, I suppose, even if you have to write a missive. I cannot imagine a note from you would be suspect."

"You are in love with her," Jasper concluded.

Geoffrey nearly naysaid him on the spot. Then it dawned on him what the pain in his chest was and why his heart felt like a solid lump of brass. He wouldn't deny he loved her.

"I believe it crucial to my future happiness that I halt any marital plans being made for Lady Caroline with that dratted Mangue."

"Agreed," Jasper said. "Life is hard. For some it's short. We shouldn't squander something as precious as love."

He spoke like a man in earnest. Geoffrey stared at him.

"Are you in love?"

Jasper shrugged. "I may have my sights set on a lucky lady." Then he grinned. "But let us deal with you first, shall we?"

CAROLINE DIDN'T THINK she could feel any more miserable, but then she heard Lord Trent's voice downstairs. Geoffrey was plainly trying to reach her despite thinking her complicit in some scheme of treachery, which she couldn't imagine.

Hardly sleeping the night before, she was torn between the wondrous sensations Geoffrey's intimate touch had elicited and the black melancholy from seeing how he looked at her after Lord Mangue arrived.

Plainly, Geoffrey thought himself betrayed, but she hoped he had come to a more sensible conclusion.

Their butler informed Lord Trent she was not accepting visitors. Caroline assumed her mother had given those instructions. She would not create an unpleasant commotion by rushing down the stairs and trying to see him against Lady Chimes's wishes.

However, as soon as he departed, Caroline descended, hoping Geoffrey's friend had at least left a note.

Her mother was in the drawing room, reading from a single sheet of paper.

At her entrance, Lady Chimes looked up, her green gaze hard as emeralds.

"I don't know what you're playing at, but I will not let you throw yourself away on Diamond."

"Throw myself away?" Caroline sputtered. "He's not a pauper or a reprobate."

Her mother pursed her lips and looked back down. "You shall not be going to Hatchards bookshop again, not until you are a happily married woman."

"Happily?" Caroline shot back. "Or merely married to anyone as long as he does not carry the name of Diamond."

"Why is Lord Trent acting as a messenger?" She waved the note she was holding. "I allowed him to dance with you in good faith and even to spend time with you at Vauxhall. Apparently, he is as unsavory as Diamond."

"Mother, please give me the letter if it was intended for me. You have no right to—"

In response, her mother turned, crumpled the page, and tossed it into the glowing hearth.

Caroline nearly darted forward to snatch it back, but she was a woman, not a child. Instead, she straightened her shoulders and lifted her chin.

"If I don't want to marry Lord Mangue, then I won't. I have your red hair, and I also have your spirit." Turning on her heel, she walked out.

With no idea when she was supposed to go to Hatchards, she couldn't meet Geoffrey. Lingering for hours in a bookseller's shop was not an option. Her other avenue of communication was Daphne. However, not wishing to bring scandal to her friend's door, she would have to tread carefully in that regard. Caroline regretted the hint of impropriety having already taken place in the Hollidge home.

Having already sent Daphne a letter of apology, Caroline would wait until she encountered her at the next assembly and hope they were still as close as sisters. Meanwhile, there was nothing she could do to further her own cause.

By dinnertime, with the delivery of the evening papers, her world had turned upside down.

Lord Chimes came from his study clutching a newspaper.

"My daughter was caught in a compromising situation at a dinner party, and I have to learn of it in *The Times*?" he demanded of his wife.

Caroline and her mother were silently seated in the drawing room, ignoring one another. She was reading the Waverly novel while her mother attempted needlepoint and doing it badly, as she always did.

At her father's words, Caroline and her mother exchanged matching wide-eyed verdant glances. Suddenly, they were on the same side of the battle, for they had both kept the truth from Lord Chimes.

That gave Caroline a small sense of satisfaction.

"I would have thought Mother might have come straight home and told you," Caroline said, sounding bored.

"What?" Lord Chimes exclaimed, rounding on his wife. "Lydia! What is our daughter saying? You *knew* about this?"

"I rescued her from Diamond's clutches," her mother said dramatically. "No one saw her, not even the hostess."

"No one except Lord Mangue," Caroline pointed out. Perhaps the man had changed his mind, and instead of marrying her, he'd decided to drag her name through the gutter as revenge.

"And Diamond," her mother said.

"Of course it was Diamond," her father spat out, sounding bitter. "I suppose he didn't like being thwarted."

Then he turned to Caroline.

"He *was* thwarted, wasn't he?"

She felt a flush of heat creep up her neck and over her face. This was a discussion she had hoped never to have with her parents.

"He *was* thwarted, Father," she insisted. *Was that the truth?* She didn't know if Geoffrey's fingers upon her counted as ruining her, but she doubted it. It must be the act of creating children that was the true destruction of a woman's virtue.

"He was thwarted!" her mother insisted. "I told you that I barged in on them. The rascal had kissed her, but that was all."

Her father sighed. Then he threw the newspaper onto the table.

"I suppose Mangue will cry off any marriage arrangement after this."

"That's convenient," Caroline said, "because I don't intend to marry the man." Furtively, she leaned forward and pulled *The Times* toward her.

"Is *your* daughter speaking to me that way?" her father asked, looking at her mother.

"Yes, dear, but she is *our* daughter after all. Would you have her be a noodle-headed namby-pamby?"

"I would have her be sensible and obedient," her father retorted. "If I go to the trouble of arranging a fine young man to marry her, I think she should be both grateful and agreeable."

"Speaking about me as if I am not in the room is intolerable," Caroline said. "If I am old enough to be married, then I am old enough to be treated as an adult and not a mischievous child. I don't find Lord Mangue to be a *fine* man, at least not fine-looking. Moreover, he has a tepid nature."

She wrinkled her nose, unable to explain why he reminded her of runny custard or tasteless blancmange while Geoffrey Diamond was like the best juicy piece of roast beef or a delicious slice of buttered toast.

"Why are you smiling then?" her father demanded.

"Merely looking forward to dinner."

"I tell you what," Lord Chimes said, "marry Mangue, if he'll still have you, and I'll add a little something extra to your dowry for your marital allowance."

"I cannot be bought," she insisted.

"It is dreadfully difficult to live a happy life without money," her mother pointed out.

"Are my own parents threatening me with penury?" Caroline asked.

There was a moment's hesitation, and then her father blinked.

"No, of course not. I was only thinking to gift you with more if you decide to be sensible."

"And if I decide to marry for love?"

"Do you fancy yourself in love with Diamond?" Lady Chimes asked. "You scarcely know him except for his dark-haired looks."

Caroline could hardly confess to how many conversations and kisses they'd actually shared. She merely shrugged.

"If he did tell *The Times* about your tryst in the pantry, then he is a blackguard," her father reminded her. "After all, it's unlikely it was Mangue unless he wants to appear a fool. Why would he blacken your name before he takes you as his wife?"

They were back to Lord Mangue. Caroline hoped he did in fact cry off because of the article in the paper, despite a ruined reputation being nothing to celebrate. Yet if Geoffrey had been the one to disclose their encounter, then she didn't want him either. Such a betrayal was the opposite of chivalry and gentlemanly behavior. It was unforgivable.

She scanned the single paragraph in the column on London's fashionable folk. While the rag-writer only vaguely referred both to her and to Geoffrey, their identities would be clear to anyone who knew the members of the *ton*.

"Young Lady C__ who chimes like a bell and Lord D__ who knows well how to ring said bell with sparkle to spare . . ."

As she came to the conclusion, she stifled a gasp.

". . . were found in a pantler's closet, where the former, a diamond of the first water, was being polished by the latter, a diamond in the rough."

Her father had handled such a titillating public denouncement very well. Frankly, she was shocked and embarrassed to be the topic of such a scandal.

Could Geoffrey be the type of person to do such a thing out of anger?

For the first time, she wondered if he was exactly like his father after all, a flagrant rake who stole other people's sweethearts and ruined them. On the other hand, his father had married Lady Diamond, thereby restoring her to respectability.

If Caroline didn't receive and accept a marriage proposal quickly, her own reputation might be irretrievably lost.

CHAPTER TEN

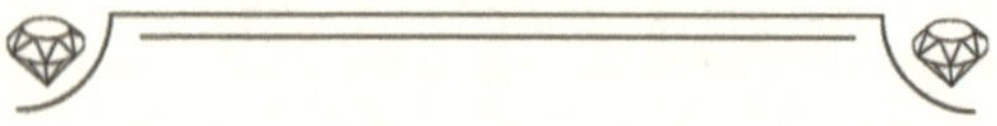

Geoffrey paced the floor of Hatchards, but Caroline never arrived. And why would she if she was perfectly happy giving her hand to Mangue? If only he knew for certain whether she had a secret *tendre* for the man.

He wasn't going to wait for another infernal ball. Instead, he loitered outside the Chimes's home the following day, not in his own carriage emblazoned with his family's coat of arms. Rather, he was in a hired hackney.

After seeing the incriminating article in *The Times*, even his own parents demanded he offer for Lady Caroline. He didn't bother to tell them his own doubts over whether her heart was already given to Mangue, or at the very least, her hand. If they thought she might be fickle, they wouldn't condone him taking her as his wife.

From his vantage point, Geoffrey saw Lord Chimes leave the residence. Stretching out his legs, he continued his vigil. If Lady Chimes left, too, then he might attempt to breach the front door. However, she never went out.

Instead, Lord Mangue arrived around noon, and Geoffrey sat up, scowling. *Had the rogue spoken to The Times in order to lower her dowry price?* That seemed the only reasonable explanation as to why Mangue would have told the newspaper about what he saw and embellished it with what he imagined.

Deciding to take the bull by the horns, Geoffrey jumped down, paid off the driver, and crossed the road. Knocking upon the door, he asked to see Lady Caroline.

"She is not receiving visitors, my lord," came the butler's reply.

"Then I would like to speak to Lady Chimes." For Geoffrey didn't give a fig with whom he met, as long as he got his foot in the door and talked to someone.

The butler sighed. "Her ladyship is also not receiving visitors."

Crossing his arms, against all standards of politeness, he said, "That's ridiculous! I can hear voices in the drawing room."

Seeing one of the double doors was ajar, he skirted the shocked butler and hurried toward it.

Sure enough, there was Lady Chimes and Lord Mangue, while Lady Caroline was nowhere in sight.

"What is the meaning of this?" Lady Chimes demanded.

"I wish to offer for your daughter," he said at once. "May I speak with Lady Caroline?"

"Here now," Mangue said, rising to his feet. "Her parents and I already have an understanding."

"You have done enough damage already," her mother added, "with that unforgiveable tattling tale to *The Times*."

"Indeed," Mangue said.

"I didn't say a word," Geoffrey vowed. "How would it benefit me? Obviously, this man did."

"I didn't. Not a peep," Mangue protested. "It would benefit me even less. You told the newspaper, so I would cease my pursuit of Lady Caroline. Obviously, *you* did it. And the proof is that you're here now."

"I am here because only by marrying her can I salvage her reputation."

"On the contrary," Lady Chimes insisted, "if Lord Mangue marries her, it will disprove the false statements. Who would believe a sane man would marry her if she were truly ruined? Ergo, Lord Mangue will marry her and remove any whiff of tainted virtue."

"And I shall receive a larger dowry for my trouble," Lord Mangue added, causing Lady Chimes to narrow her eyes at him.

"We were discussing it," she said firmly, "but no decision can be made until I've discussed it with my husband."

"I will take Lady Caroline without any dowry at all," Geoffrey offered, as if he were bidding on horseflesh at Tattersall's.

Both of them stared at him, mouths slightly open.

"Not if you betrayed me to *The Times*," Caroline said from the doorway. "In which case, I shall have nothing to do with you."

Geoffrey felt a shard of warmth slice through him like summer sunshine, simply from seeing her. Moreover, he couldn't help smiling.

"How dare you grin at my daughter?" Lady Chimes said.

"How can I not?" he asked. "She is perfection."

"What poppycock!" Mangue muttered. "If Diamond doesn't want a dowry, he'll probably be miserly with his wife, keep her in rags, and not give her any pin money."

"Nonsense. My wife may have all my fortune," Geoffrey insisted. "I will rest it at her feet."

Instead of garnering a smile in return from Caroline, she frowned.

"I want to hear the answer. Did *you* speak with *The Times*?"

"No," he said firmly.

She looked at Mangue. "Did *you* talk to *The Times*?"

"Indubitably not," he said, sounding sincere. Even Geoffrey couldn't doubt him.

"Then I am entirely bewildered for I know it was not I nor my mother." Caroline looked at Mangue. "Only know, my lord, I think it the height of kindness that you would still offer for my hand."

"I want your hand," Geoffrey interrupted, "and not out of kindness."

They stared at one another.

Her mother bristled. "You will leave, Lord Diamond, or I will have our butler toss you out."

Geoffrey tried to imagine the Chimes's butler achieving such a feat, but it didn't matter. He wouldn't create such an ignominious scene. That was, not unless Caroline asked him to stay.

"I came to see you, Lady Caroline, to pledge my troth and to ask for your hand."

"You are out of line," Lady Chimes said, but Geoffrey didn't turn his gaze from her daughter's exquisite face.

"I will gladly help your butler get rid of this rascal," Mangue offered.

Geoffrey heard him but ignored his words, waiting only for an answer from Caroline.

She stared at him a long moment before glancing at her mother.

"Don't you dare respond to this scoundrel," Lady Chimes directed. "His behavior is beyond the pale!"

Caroline bit her lower lip, which he found not only charming but incredibly arousing.

"I don't believe I shall marry either one of you," she said finally.

While he was digesting that odd statement, she turned heel and left.

GEOFFREY HAD TO ENDURE first one week and then two of missing Caroline. He had not simply enjoyed each of their brief, furtive encounters, he had relished them. She'd become a necessary part of his existence, even if he'd had to hide his affection and disguise his admiration. Yet she disappeared from the events on the Season's social calendar and cut off all contact.

He sent notes on three occasions, left his calling card twice, and even demanded to see her to an utterly impassive butler—all to no avail. Either she had lost interest, or her parents were keeping her on a tight rein.

And then one day, she appeared again. He was at the theatre with a young lady whose mother was a friend of his own mother. His companion was attractive, soft-spoken, and had a sweet smile, but she wasn't Caroline. It wasn't the lady's fault that he couldn't muster up the enthusiasm to even sniff her hair or do anything more than politely smile.

While he was looking out over the audience from his family's box during the intermission, having been a terrible escort and declining to go to the lobby for wine and jabbering prattle, he saw a head of glorious red hair. Paired with another equally coppery-headed female, he knew in a heartbeat it must be Caroline and her mother.

Leaning forward, he tried to see the rest of their party. He spied Lord Chimes, too, and hoped Caroline was with only her parents, but then she leaned over to speak to the man at her left and even laid her hand upon his arm. With their heads bent close, they spoke and then laughed.

Geoffrey's insides tightened as a burst of jealousy raced through him. *Dammit all!*

"Are you well, my lord?" asked the lady beside him. "You groaned and muttered."

He wanted to tell her he felt bloody awful and do the unforgivable—take her home before the evening's entertainment ended. However, his mother would give him hell if he offended her friend's daughter.

"My apologies. A touch of indigestion is all." He rolled his eyes at his ridiculous words, making himself sound like an old man with gout. Glad when the lamps dimmed, so he could no longer see Caroline and her escort, who appeared a damn sight more appealing than Mangue, Geoffrey settled back for the longest evening of his life.

He would not make the same mistake. He would remain a monk rather than be tortured by being in the company of a hapless miss who could do nothing but disappoint him through no fault of her own. She was simply the wrong woman.

Thus, the rest of the Season passed without him in attendance.

He didn't want to see Caroline, so he stayed away from the ballrooms. Despite his self-imposed banishment, he read the daily papers, dreading the appearance of an engagement announcement between her and Mangue or even with the mysterious stranger. Luckily, there were none.

Waiting did nothing to further his own pursuit of her, and while the passage of time gave tongues other scandals to wag on about, it did little to lessen Geoffrey's obsession with the red-haired goddess. Finally, it was Stir-Up Sunday, the last Sunday before the season of Advent, and he was at his parents' home for a long-held tradition.

"This has seemed an exceedingly long year," James Diamond said, rubbing his hands as he stood before the hearth in their drawing room. "Parliament has been busy. We started a new war with the Burmese, which I think shall drag on and be damnably expensive. Regrettably, it had to be done."

He took his glass of brandy from the mantel and sipped.

"On the other hand, I personally helped create a few acts that hopefully shall prove useful, and we signed a good treaty with the Dutch."

The Earl Diamond loved when they had a peaceful accord rather than a ruinous war. But Geoffrey was in no mood for good news.

"From the sublime to the ridiculous, our government stopped a war, started one, and spent a fortune on Angerstien's art collection," he said, feeling dour despite the normally festive occasion.

This custom of discussing their year on Stir-Up Sunday had begun when he'd been sent away to school. Upon his return for the long winter break, they would enjoy recapping what each had done, with the comforting knowledge that in their well-staffed kitchen the Christmas puddings were being made as they traditionally were on this day. For the next month, the liquor-soaked puddings would cure until they were brought to the table on Christmas day.

"With Angerstien's collection, we now have a public art gallery," his mother reminded him. "I think it's wonderful and worth every penny. If my loving husband wishes to commission a painting of me before I lose my looks, then I shall donate it."

"I shall do so in the new year at the earliest instant," the earl promised. "As soon as I find the best painter."

Lady Diamond narrowed her eyes. "Why the rush, husband? Are you saying I am already in danger of showing my age?"

When his father threw him a desperate look, Geoffrey merely shrugged. Let the man get himself out of it.

"Not at all, my love," Lord Diamond said. "But you cannot fault me for wanting the public to be able to enjoy your likeness on canvas as soon as humanly possible."

Marianne Diamond smiled and lifted her glass of wine in agreement.

Geoffrey ignored them. The new National Gallery, as it was known, only reminded him of seeing Caroline there before their debacle at the Hollidge dinner party. Her mother had kept him at bay.

"I sat in on the founding of the Society for the Prevention of Cruelty to Animals," his father continued to boast his list of accomplishments. "I was invited to Old Slaughter's Coffee House by the Reverend Broome himself and am proud of our members of parliament who sat with me for such a worthy cause."

"A good thing, too," Lady Diamond said. "There is no reason to strike a dog or a horse."

"No more than one would strike a woman," the earl agreed. "Poor creatures."

"Women or animals?" the countess quipped.

They laughed.

Geoffrey didn't join in and thought he ought to have stayed home this year and avoided the family tradition, especially since his biggest accomplishment was failing to gain the hand of the woman he loved. And he could hardly share that since he would garner no sympathy with his parents for the loss of a Chimes as his wife.

Nevertheless, he knew how to put a damper on their fun.

"As a nation, we hosted the King and Queen of the Sandwich Islands," he said. "Hosted them right into an early grave."

"Geoffrey!" his mother exclaimed. "How could anyone know they would catch the measles so easily? Besides, they had a wonderful time before they got sick."

"Got sick and *died*, Mother, far from home. What's more, the king was a year younger than I am."

"Still," she said, "they enjoyed the opera at Covent Garden."

"And you saw them at the Theatre Royal, didn't you?" his father asked him. "I saw the king myself, tall chap."

Geoffrey had seen King Kamehameha before he fell sick without ever getting an audience with King George. *Poor man!* But that night, Geoffrey had also seen Caroline with her parents. Again, that had been when his future still seemed as if it might have her in it. She'd looked beautiful, and he'd watched her instead of the stage. She had even discreetly waved at him in the dimly lit auditorium.

"The king and queen couldn't have done any of the entertaining things they did in London," Lady Diamond pointed out, "if they'd stayed on their little island."

"Island*s*, Mother. It's a chain of them. Never mind." Geoffrey shook his head. His mother was indeed frivolous. Apparently, she thought coming to London to see the opera and meet a bunch of noblemen had been worth their lives.

"Come now, think of something happier," Marianne Diamond insisted.

"Lord Byron died," Geoffrey said. At least the adventuresome baron had lived life to the fullest and known more than his share of passionate love, too, if all the newspaper recounts were true.

"I said *happier*," his mother reminded him. "Poor foolish man!"

She might as well have been speaking of her own son as of Byron. For Geoffrey was foolish through and through to have thought Lady Caroline genuinely cared about him.

He still wasn't sure whether she'd merely been exacting revenge on him for her parents' sake. It had seemed so when she cavalierly said she didn't wish to marry him and left the room. He remembered the moment as if it had been yesterday.

Geoffrey imagined it was why she'd allowed him to take liberties, too.

Now that Stir-Up Sunday was done and dusted, they would hurtle swiftly toward Christmas and the new year. Strange how he'd been all but certain he would have proposed to a willing wife by now.

The following day, he met Jasper at White's and endured another cheering-up similar to what his parents had attempted, although they were ignorant of the reason for his fit of the blue devils that would not abate. With Jasper, he could speak plainly.

"I haven't seen Lady Caroline for months. Yet sometimes, it seems as if I've seen her quite recently—she is still so clear before my mind's eye."

"Saw her and kissed her," Jasper added.

"And kissed her," he agreed.

Geoffrey had no wish to continue moping and feeling sorry for himself. Nevertheless, it was hard to disabuse his heart and his brain of the notion that he had found the one woman who suited him best in every regard. Even less did he have enthusiasm for hunting another, knowing she would be second best.

With his fist, he hit the linen-covered table, making Jasper jump as well as some of the other diners nearby.

"I can't stand this another minute," Geoffrey vowed. "I tell you she is mine and meant to be. She said she would not marry me, but I ought to have tried harder."

"Harder than the notes, flowers, and getting the Chimes's door slammed in your face?"

"Yes, harder. She is worth it. And I didn't ever try flowers. That seemed a tad sappy, frankly."

Jasper shrugged. "Do you have a plan?"

"Actually, yes, I do." Geoffrey could think of only one plan, clichéd as it was. "You provided it to me with your talk of *Romeo and Juliet* months ago."

CHAPTER ELEVEN

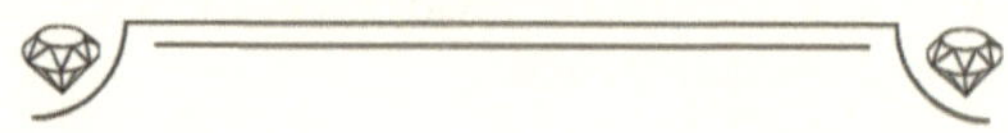

"I appreciate your help," Geoffrey told Jasper before they dropped as silently as possible over the garden wall. Landing on the coal bin had been unexpected, making a clattering sound that caused them to remain motionless, holding their breath. When no one opened the back door, they moved forward.

Although Jasper wasn't so much helping as offering friendly support, agreeing to be a lookout or a second in a duel if it came to it.

At White's, his friend had been nonchalant. "We shall go to her home tonight, and I vow you will speak with her," Jasper said as if sneaking around after dark were the most natural thing in the world for a couple of titled bucks. "Like men of derring-do."

And now Geoffrey found himself hiding behind a tree in the Chimes's back garden, feeling more foolish than daring. On the other hand, he would be happy to escape without a lead ball fired into his body, so Geoffrey supposed there was some measure of actual danger.

"I don't suppose you know which is your lady's bedchamber," Jasper asked.

"How would I know that?" Geoffrey asked. *Was his friend casting aspersions on Caroline?*

"Don't get into a high tweague, Diamond. But it would be damn useful if you knew which window."

Jasper was right. But over brandy, going there at two in the morning had seemed like a good idea and an easy one.

"Would it be better to break in the back door and roam the house?" his friend wondered aloud while staring at the upper floors.

While Geoffrey thought he might meet with better success indoors than climbing a tree or a trellis and knocking on Lord and Lady Chimes's window by mistake, it was also riskier. He could get sent to jail for breaking in like a thieving *fidlam ben*.

"If she were my daughter, I would have her room away from the street, I suppose," he guessed.

"But not at the very back of the house," Jasper added. "In case any nefarious nobleman wanted to use an apple tree to climb in her window."

Geoffrey sighed. This was a bone-headed plan. Luckily, the Chimes's had a corner home, so he could explore the side of the house as easily as the back.

"I'm going to guess that window." He pointed above them.

Jasper handed him a rock.

"If I'm wrong," Geoffrey said, "prepare to bolt like a skittish deer."

Setting his lantern upon the ground, he hefted the rock in his hand.

"I believe it's supposed to be a few small pebbles, enough to make a noise but not break the glass. Give me something smaller," he demanded.

"If you hit the house, not the glass, it will be fine," Jasper insisted.

"That won't awaken her. I need pebbles," he insisted. "Maybe I could toss coins. That would make a goodly racket."

"I don't think you should throw anything directly at the glass," Jasper said.

Dropping the rock, he searched in his pockets and withdrew some coppers.

"Perfect. Stand by, Trent."

"I am, Diamond. I am."

"Very well." He jiggled the coins a moment as if he were shaking dice.

"Let them fly," Jasper said encouragingly.

"I was about to. Stop talking."

Taking a step back, he tossed them at the window he'd chosen just as the sash lifted.

"OH!" CAROLINE EXCLAIMED as a handful of coins hit her in the face and chest. *What the devil?*

"My apologies," came Geoffrey's voice as he bent to retrieve his lantern. "Are you injured?"

As the frigid air swirled into her room, she peered into the side garden. *Was he in his cups?*

"Who is with you?" she asked, seeing another figure beside him.

"'Tis I, Lord Trent," came a cheerful voice, and to prove it, he lifted his lantern up to his face.

"A moment," she said, wondering if she were still asleep and dreaming.

Hurrying to light a lamp, she snatched up her thick wool dressing gown and wrapped it around herself. Having been awakened by voices, she had lifted the sash at precisely the wrong instant.

Returning to the window, she heard Lord Trent exclaim, "What light through yonder window breaks."

"Quiet," she pleaded. If her parents weren't already awake, they would be. And that would bring this unexpected farce to a hasty end.

On the other hand, knowing Geoffrey was mere feet away, for the first time in weeks, she felt happiness drizzle like a gentle rain upon her.

"Yes, do muzzle yourself," Geoffrey added. Then he looked up. "I need to speak with you."

"Come closer and speak softly," she said.

They both shuffled forward, but then Geoffrey waved his friend away. "Stay back, for God's sake," he ordered.

"Only trying to help," Lord Trent replied, but then he and his lantern disappeared toward the wall.

Geoffrey began again. "I am sorry to awaken you and to hit you with coins."

Her heart melted at his awkward beginning.

"After what you said about not marrying me, I had to discern the true depths of your feelings. I must know what's in your heart."

She caught her breath. Perhaps he was the terrible rogue her parents believed him to be, for it was inconceivable he could ask her to state plainly such an intimate thing. And how unwise for her to tell him that she loved him. If he knew, it would put her in a terribly vulnerable position.

In the end, all she said was, "Why?"

"Why?" he repeated. "I assume you are asking why I wish to know."

"Yes, exactly."

"Because you have moved into my heart and taken up all the space."

Then they were as twins. *How brave of him to confess that to her.*

"Your silence makes me exceedingly nervous," he said. "Moreover, I saw you with an unfamiliar man at the theatre."

She leaned a little farther out, wishing she could be down in the garden with him, but it was too dangerous to try to sneak past her parents' room and down the stairs.

Taking a deep, chilly breath, Caroline decided to tell him. Either she would be as happy as her best friend Daphne, who had long since forgiven her for sullying her pantry, or she would become as forlorn as Shakespeare's doomed Juliet, to whom Lord Trent had just alluded.

"I love you," she confessed.

When he said nothing, Caroline's heart began to pound. *What was he thinking?* That this was a turning point in their lives, or maybe he was pondering the impossibility of their situation given the animosity between their parents.

When she was about to demand he tell her his thoughts, he spoke.

"I wish someone had thought to put a strong rose trellis here or planted a sturdy tree with branches touching your window. I love you, and I swear I would be up there beside you in a twitch of a lamb's tail if I could."

Relief poured through her, and she closed her eyes with a long sigh.

"Will you marry me, Lady Caroline Chimes?"

Her eyes popped open. "If I could, Geoffrey Diamond, I would." It was as honest as she could be.

He stared up at her.

"And you don't actually long for Mangue?"

"I promise you, I do not. I was stunned when I found out that my parents had spoken to him about marrying me. I should have told you."

She wouldn't be so petty as to discuss his mercenary tendency in requesting a larger dowry, for he must be a decent man to wish to marry her despite the ugly rumors.

"I see." Another pause, and then he added, "I have already told you in front of your mother that I wish to marry you," Geoffrey reminded her. "That has not changed in all these weeks."

"Did you tell *The Times* about the butler's pantry?" she asked, needing to know.

"I swear I did not."

"I did," came Lord Trent's voice out of the darkness, proving he had been listening all along.

"What?" Geoffrey roared.

"*Sshh,*" she admonished.

"You said you wanted to do whatever it took to break up an arrangement between Mangue and your lady," Lord

Trent explained. "But I knew you to be too honorable to actually follow through."

Stunned silence met his statement, and then Geoffrey's disbelieving exclamation, "You tattled to the newspapers!"

Caroline tried to imagine what Geoffrey had told his friend of their intimate encounter and felt her cheeks heat even with the cool night air streaming against her.

"I made up a story based on the little you told me," Lord Trent said. "It helped, didn't it?"

"I would punch you if you weren't my best friend," Geoffrey growled.

"Gentlemen," she said to regain their attention. "I think it was a terrible idea, but what's done is done. My parents think only marrying Lord Mangue will erase the stain upon my reputation. For you see, if he marries me, it will plainly demonstrate that nothing really happened."

"Oh!" came Lord Trent's voice again. "I hadn't thought of that, only of driving Mangue and his extraordinary eyebrow away."

She would have laughed if it weren't all so serious.

"I don't care," Geoffrey said. "Marry me, and we'll weather any storm."

"You don't know what it might mean," she said, although like sunshine between the clouds, a shard of hope broke through the heavy doubt and melancholy that had dogged her.

Then to her amazement, Geoffrey laughed.

"Dearest Caroline," he said. "Do you forget who my parents are, and what my father has long been reputed to have done? More than anyone, I understand what this could mean. And still, I don't give a fig. We shall not be shunned, I promise you. If anything, it lifted my parents into a mythological realm of desperate, undeniable love."

Caroline considered his words. *Desperate, undeniable love*— that was a perfect description for what she felt.

"Besides," he added, "any blame has been laid at my father's feet as a bit of a rake. Even then, he is widely forgiven because he married my mother, and they've stayed together without anyone ever being able to say either has been unfaithful."

It was true that she'd only ever heard any fault being placed on Lord Diamond, except where her parents were concerned. Lady Diamond was considered an unwilling victim, and also a perfectly lovely and lucky countess who snared an earl.

"Please marry me," he said again, his tone causing a lump in her throat.

"How?" she asked even as her pulse fluttered. She might actually get to marry the only man who had ever made her shiver.

"I spoke in jest once about Gretna Green," he reminded her. "Now I believe we ought to take our chances. The alternative is to wait a year until you don't need anyone's permission."

A wretched long year of being berated, scolded, pushed, and coerced.

"I think a border wedding sounds wonderful," she agreed. "When?"

She half expected him to say, "Now," which would have put her into a panicky rub. She wanted to bathe with her favorite floral soap, pack a bag, choose the perfect gown, and tell Daphne the thrilling news.

Nevertheless, if he said it had to be that instant or wait for the reign of Queen Dick, as her father would say to mean never at all, then she would dress in the first gown she had at hand and slip outside to meet him. Or more romantically, she could drop into his awaiting arms.

Gauging the distance, Caroline hoped she didn't end up with a broken neck.

Luckily, Geoffrey needed time to plan, too.

"Can you go to Lady Hollidge's tomorrow around ten o'clock? I shall meet you there with enough funds for our journey, and we shall take flight directly."

Just eight hours! Caroline had trouble catching her breath. She was going to do something she had never considered possible—*elopement!* Some thought it a starry-eyed endeavor. Most knew it was the stuff of foolish girls and greedy, wicked men. But she was no fool, and Geoffrey was not after her money.

Yet even if she could get ready in time, which she would, her mother would question her sanity at going out visiting at such an impolite hour.

"Eleven would be better, for the sake of civility," she said.

"Very well. I will be at Lady Hollidge's home five minutes before eleven."

In the glow of his lantern, she could see his handsome grin, and her heart clenched.

"I love you," he said, surprising her.

More than ever, she wished she were in his arms instead of hanging over the casement.

"I love you, too," she told him, no longer the least bit embarrassed.

"Parting is such sweet sorrow," quipped Lord Trent, whom she'd entirely forgotten.

"Shut your gob!" Geoffrey ordered. And then the two men disappeared into the shadows.

Caroline sighed and, with frozen fingers, closed the window sash. She knew she would not sleep, nor could she ask the staff for a bath or do anything out of the ordinary until morning. Belatedly, she realized it would have been smart of her to toss a sack down to Geoffrey containing clothing, for she would not be able to leave in the morning with anything except her reticule.

In fact, knowing she would have to hide her excitement from her clever mother, she decided to take breakfast in her room and stay there until the last possible moment.

Even when her maid was delivering the requested hot chocolate and toast to her room, Caroline was still toying with the notion of wearing a second dress under her day gown, but if her mother should see her leave, it would be all too obvious.

Unless she put on her fur-trimmed redingote while still in her room.

"Bring my winter coat up here," she asked her maid. "I'm going out in an hour, and I'll get bundled up before I go downstairs."

Her maid looked at her, probably wondering why Caroline was prattling on and explaining herself. She offered the young woman a smile and sent her on her way. And then, as she was wondering which of her prettier dresses would best fit under what she was wearing, something she would be proud to be seen in even for an anvil wedding, there was a knock at her door.

She knew that knock. Only her mother's knuckles made that particular rapping sound.

Glancing around the room, she began to shove the dresses from her bed into her wardrobe, knowing it to be a hopeless task.

Her plan for a speedy escape was already in ruins.

CHAPTER TWELVE

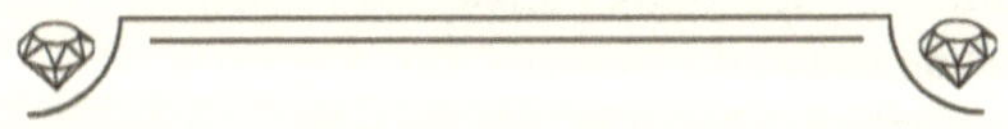

"Caroline, are you awake and dressed?"

"Yes, Mother." Drat! *Why hadn't she said she was feeling ill and had decided to sleep in?*

With that answer, her mother felt it her place to open the door and stroll in. And thus, Caroline was discovered with an arm full of gowns.

"What on earth are you doing?"

What was she doing? Caroline could barely come up with the simplest excuse.

"I was bored and decided to look through my dresses and see if I should consider having any altered." With that, she dumped them back on the bed.

"Your poor maid will have quite a time tidying all that up," her mother said. "If you're bored, why don't you come with me? I'm going to the new National Gallery."

"We've already been," Caroline reminded her.

"Darling, you don't go once to a museum and consider it finished. You go again and again to study the paintings and remark upon them."

"Some people go to see who is there and to be seen admiring great art," Caroline said, hoping to dissuade her mother with the intimation it was a vulgar outing.

Her mother shook her head. "That sounds rather shallow. Something Lady Diamond might do. In fact, she's probably trying to figure out how to get her own portrait onto the wall." Then her mother frowned. "Are you well?"

"Yes, why?" Caroline realized she'd gasped aloud.

"You paled suddenly."

"Did I?" She'd been startled beyond reason by her mother mentioning the name of Diamond.

"And now you look flushed. Sit down."

Caroline did as her mother said, finding a spot between the gowns just as there came a knock at the door.

"Come in," her mother answered for her.

Caroline's maid entered carrying her dark green redingote with its soft gray fur trim.

"Why have you brought that up here?" Lady Chimes demanded.

"Lady Caroline asked me to, my lady."

Both pairs of eyes stared at her, and Caroline took a step back.

"I was going out because… as I said, I was bored, and I . . . I thought seeing how it is cold, I would don my coat and hat while in the warmth of my room."

"Where were you going?" her mother asked.

"Merely for a walk."

"Then I shall accompany you. I can go to the museum later if you still don't wish to go. I suppose some fresh air is a good idea, as long as we don't stay out too long and risk catching a chill."

GEOFFREY PACED LADY Hollidge's drawing room, but after waiting an hour and a half, it was obvious Caroline was not coming.

Had she changed her mind?

"My lord, I fear something has detained her," Daphne Hollidge said, stating the obvious while bouncing her little boy on her lap.

Geoffrey feared it was not something but *someone*. He eyed the young Alexander Hollidge, knowing the boy wanted his mother's attention. The totiken had arrived about twenty minutes earlier after awakening from a nap. And when he did, he'd made enough noise while entering with his nanny that Geoffrey had been sure Caroline had at last arrived.

He could not know for certain whether it was Caroline's disinclination to elope that had stopped her or an external factor. He prayed it was the latter.

"I am sorry to have disrupted your household today and to have wasted your time," he said, wondering if he would be spending another evening tossing coins at Caroline's window to obtain an explanation.

A noise in the foyer snagged both of their attention.

"Daphne, is he still here?" came Caroline's voice, and then she appeared in the doorway.

Her hat was askew, her cheeks were pink with exertion as if she'd been running, and she never looked lovelier.

"*Oh!*" she exclaimed upon seeing him, and then she burst into tears.

Not caring that Lady Hollidge would bear witness, Geoffrey rushed to claim her and wrap her in his arms. She collapsed against him.

"What's happened? Are you well?"

"My mother thwarted me at every turn. I fear she suspects something since, in the middle of Hyde Park, I finally declared I needed to be alone and rushed straight here."

"I shall order a pot of tea," Lady Hollidge said. "Do sit and try to catch your breath."

Caroline's lovely gaze looked up at him. "Do we have time? Have I ruined everything?"

Geoffrey tried to calm his racing heart. She was in his arms, and she still wanted to elope with him. Everything was fine again.

"We should begin our journey. It will take three days if we don't kill the horses. You'll have plenty of time to sit, I assure you."

"I have nothing with me. I couldn't leave home with a bag."

Lady Hollidge instantly became their angel. "Take tea, please, Caroline. While you do, I shall have a trunk packed at once with everything you'll need."

"Dear Daphne. How can I ever repay you?"

"We are like sisters, are we not?" She was already heading for the door. "Catch your breath. Tea will arrive in five minutes, and I vow I will have you out the door in fifteen."

As good as her word, Lady Hollidge sent them swiftly on their way, and Caroline was a good deal calmer than when she'd stumbled in.

"My friend is so thoughtful," she said when they were passing Shoreditch Church. "She even gave me a novel and some biscuits and cake." She was digging in the carpet bag that had been pressed into her hands after a trunk was stowed on top of Geoffrey's travel coach.

"Her husband is equally kind. I hope you will enjoy their company as much as I do," she added.

Geoffrey nodded. "Gaining a wife and two friends into the bargain! And I hope, despite Lord Trent's failings, you come to like him, too. He's been a good friend to me for years."

"Maybe we shall gain yet another friend," she mused, "for he has his sights set upon Miss Holcombe, a pretty brunette."

Geoffrey was astounded. He had heard nothing about it. "How on earth do you know that?"

She smiled. "I have kept my eyes open all Season. Mostly, I was looking for you. But when you were not in sight, I noticed other people."

He laughed. "Will you sit beside me?" He patted the leather seat.

"Will you behave yourself?" she asked, tilting her head, beaming with happiness.

He could only promise he would try, but the unusual circumstance of being in a carriage alone with a beautiful woman without a chaperone was titillating beyond all measure.

Moreover, in light of what they were doing, her question gave him pause.

"You know it no longer matters what we do or do not do. We are alone, and thus you are irreparably ruined."

She wrinkled her adorable nose. "A horrid word."

"But you understand we shall be spending two or possibly three nights staying at coaching inns. Even if we have separate rooms, which you should demand of me, it shall make no difference to what others will say and conclude."

"I know," she agreed quietly. "I am ruined."

"But you shall be my wife and one day a countess. I believe when we return as a wedded couple, as long as we behave with decorum, the scourge of our disgrace will disappear."

"Eventually," she agreed.

"Soon," he corrected.

"Unless we have a child too quickly."

Geoffrey's heart sped up at the realization she was already contemplating swiving, which was practically all he could think about. He didn't like to consider himself a randy dog, but he hadn't enjoyed any female company in his bed since the night he slammed into Caroline Chimes.

"Luckily," he said, "that won't be the case. Even if we . . ." He trailed off when faced with her curious green gaze.

"Yes?" she prompted.

"Even if we share a room tonight, which you should insist we do not, and even if we marry in three days, the baby will be born at the right time."

"True enough." Without another word, she lifted the thick wool blanket under which she'd been keeping warm and changed her place, nestling beside him.

He put his arm around her shoulders.

"I am sorry," she said, straightening. "This is all wrong."

Geoffrey tensed. If she'd changed her mind, he would probably throw himself out of the moving carriage over a well-placed cliff if he could find one.

"I need to sit facing the way we travel."

He breathed a sigh of relief. Many people felt a stomach upset when riding backward, including his own mother.

They rearranged themselves and faced forward, snuggling under the covering.

"Much better," Caroline said. Once again, she rested her head upon his shoulder.

"I confess I barely slept last night. And then after the excitement of the morning, I believe I could doze off if you didn't think me too rude."

"Please, take a journey to the land of Nod if you can. Maybe I shall join you. My driver and footman will alert us if there is any trouble whatsoever."

As she rested her hand on his chest, his heart bloomed with love, and he thought nothing could be better than having her start snoring gently in his arms.

Until that night when she told him to obtain a single room.

As he descended from the carriage to speak to the innkeeper, she reached out and laid her hand upon his arm.

"After all," she said, "I consider myself already your wife in all but the formality."

Her trust in him shook Geoffrey. When he had secured them the best room and were now discussing going downstairs to dinner or having it brought up to their room, he couldn't help telling her what was on his mind.

"I am actually concerned for you."

"What do you mean?" She had been removing her outer coat but now stopped to look at him, her pretty lips parted in a smile.

"You are too trusting. What if you were here with a rogue? You can't tell a man you already consider yourself married. What if I tupped you and left you here?" He was working himself up into righteous outrage on her behalf.

Instead of understanding the gravity of her circumstances, Caroline laughed and finished shrugging out of her coat, which she laid over the end of the bed. Approaching him, she put her hands up to take his face between her slender fingers.

"Geoffrey Diamond, are you going to tup me tonight?"

Swallowing hard at the instant image of fornication that sprang into his brain while his staff sprang to hard arousal as well, he stared into her unfathomable green eyes and could speak only the truth.

"Probably. In fact, certainly. Yes, I intend to." He stopped babbling as she stroked her thumb over his lower lip.

"And are you going to leave me here afterward as a fallen woman? Or will we continue our journey to Scotland, so we can marry in haste and enjoy our lives at leisure?"

"That is not how the saying goes," he pointed out. "Regardless, I am never going to leave you anywhere but stay always by your side."

She nodded, went up on tiptoe, and kissed him full upon his lips.

Before he could wrap his arms around her, however, she had broken contact and slipped past him.

"I am famished," she said. "If we are going to get to swiving later, then I need to eat now."

CHAPTER THIRTEEN

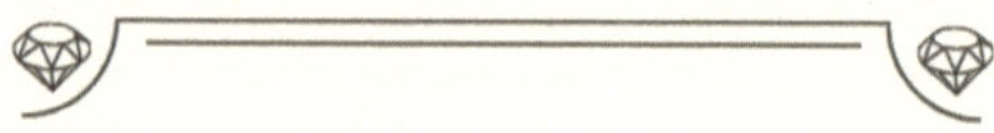

Lord James Diamond decided his son was a chip off the old block. First the episode in the butler's pantry that all of London had read about, and now it seemed Geoffrey had absconded with the willing Chimes wench.

If there was any doubt, it evaporated when he witnessed Lord and Lady Chimes barging across his foyer as soon as his butler admitted them. Allowing them in was probably a mistake, but the alternative was cowardly.

And James was no coward. Caught on the staircase, he called behind him.

"Dearest wife, we have visitors." *Intruders, more like*, he added silently.

"The Fenwicks?" Marianne called back. "I hope."

"Alas, no," he sighed. "Do hurry." And he went down to greet the least likely of guests.

"I pray you know where your rapscallion son is," Lord Chimes began.

"Good evening," James replied, ignoring the man's tone. "There is a lady present, so we shall adhere to all manner of civility. Lady Chimes, would you care for a glass of wine, given the hour?" It was that between time after dinner and before supper.

"No," she said, and James could see it cost her to finish politely, "thank you. We are here because our daughter has disappeared. And we fear she is with your son."

James wasn't done with playing host despite not fearing anything. Rather, he knew with certainty because that's what he would do if he fancied a forbidden lady. And also, because he had run into his son's best friend, Lord Trent, at White's.

"It sounds as if we have trouble brewing, and that's always better handled with brandy." Yanking the bellpull, he offered once again. "What about you, Chimes? Are you thirsty?"

"I wouldn't drink with you if you were the last man on earth."

"Rather harsh," James muttered.

Luckily, Lady Diamond entered before he could make matters worse. And then she proceeded to do precisely that.

Upon taking one look at their guests, she announced, "Our offspring have eloped."

"You knew about this?" Lady Chimes asked.

"About what?" his wife asked, infuriating their guests.

"About what?" Lord Chimes repeated. "About the elopement, of course."

"Not at all," Lady Diamond said, exasperated. "I'm not clairvoyant. Yet our son has gone away unexpectedly and then, here you are. What else can I conclude? In fact, when he didn't turn up to dinner as expected, I said to my husband, our son has probably run away with that pretty, red-headed girl. Didn't I, my love?"

"You did," he agreed, then turned to the Chimes. "She honestly did. And I told her I had heard as much at my club from a gentleman with close ties to our son. And now you've confirmed it. Do you understand now?"

He was playing the devil but couldn't stop himself.

On the other hand, his wife appeared resolved to be a hostess. "Diamond, have you offered our visitors wine?"

"Yes, my love, and brandy, but they refused," he told her.

Turning her smile upon them, he didn't know how anyone could resist Marianne's charm. "How about tea, then?" she asked.

"We don't want anything," Lady Chimes insisted in clipped tones, "except our daughter."

"Well, *we* don't have her," Lady Diamond told them. And then she took a seat, and James realized she'd come to the end of her graciousness already. She did have a rather short rope and little tolerance for anything unpleasant.

"It was careless of you to let her wander away from home unsupervised, don't you think?" she added.

James wished his countess hadn't said that. Sure enough, fireworks ensued.

"Let her *wander!*" Lord Chimes spluttered.

"More like she was snatched," Lady Chimes put in, but she also took a seat.

James didn't like that insinuation one bit. "Are you stating you believe our son kidnapped your daughter?"

"Poppycock!" Marianne said.

"Caroline was perfectly content this morning," Lady Chimes insisted. "We took a walk. There was no hint of her leaving. She didn't even have luggage!"

"If they are together, and it seems likely they are," James said, "then they are in a carriage on the best road to the closest Scottish town."

"Gretna Green," Lord Chimes interrupted.

"However, if I take my best horse," James continued, "then I may be able to beat them there."

"You mean *I* might," Lord Chimes corrected. "For I intend to go after my daughter."

"Not without me," Lady Chimes insisted. "She might be frightened or in a dreadful circumstance if your dastardly son has had his way with her."

"Then I shall go, too," Marianne insisted. "If your daughter is trying to ensnare my boy, then he'll need me to see through her feminine wiles. His heart will be broken."

"Ridiculous," Lady Chimes insisted. "Your son is obviously just like his father."

"Meaning?" Marianne asked tightly.

"Not a gentleman at all. Rather, he's willing to ruin a woman to secure her hand."

"And your daughter is just like you," Marianne said, rising once more. "A grasping mushroom!"

"How dare you!" Lady Chimes exploded, jumping to her feet. "We can't all be fickle, shallow females, tempting men in order to secure an engagement."

Marianne laughed. "Well, which is it? Did my husband ruin me or did I tempt him?"

"I thought we were talking about my daughter and your son," Lord Chimes said. "I fail to see how your sordid history is important." Even he seemed disconcerted by the turn which the conversation had taken.

"I suppose we ought to stop the wedding," James said, "at least until we sort out a marriage contract and your daughter's dowry."

Lord Chimes turned red. "Not another penny from me to you," he declared.

"We don't want to negotiate a marriage arrangement," Lady Chimes said. "We want to stop them getting married. I'm going, too, but not all that way on horseback."

"Neither am I," Marianne said. "Not when we have a comfortable traveling coach."

"As do we," Lady Chimes said, with a tilt of her chin.

"Why don't you ladies go together?" James suggested. "Then when we find them, you'll both be there should either one of our offspring need comforting or support."

It sounded ridiculous, but he knew neither of the women would want to be left behind. Nor could he allow his wife to undertake such a journey alone.

"And we shall go on horseback," Lord Chimes said, glancing at James, "to intercept them."

"Will you ride straight through?" Lady Diamond asked. "How exciting and utterly exhausting!"

"We cannot stay alone in coaching inns," Lady Chimes pointed out. "Can we?"

"We cannot stay with you," Lord Chimes pointed out, "or we might as well be in the blasted carriage, and we'll never make up time enough to catch them."

"I'll send the ladies with my driver and two footmen," James proposed. "The driver is very experienced and will know where it's safe for them to stay. And all three will be fully armed."

"I shall have to go home and pack," Lady Chimes said.

"I won't wait," Lady Diamond threatened. "Every minute wasted—"

James hated to gainsay his wife. It would mean a frosty reception in the marital bed when next he reached for her. However, since they would be apart for a few nights, she might soften toward him and forgive him by the time they met up again. Thus, he suggested a compromise.

"Dearest, I think you should give Lady Chimes leave to go home with her husband and pack what she needs. The two of you can depart at first light when you collect her in our carriage. Meanwhile, I'll have my horse saddled and some provisions put in my saddlebags and be away within the half-hour."

Lord Chimes huffed. "I need to go get my best runner. Will you head out without me or wait at Hick's Hall?"

"If I see you, we'll ride together," James said, not making any promises.

CAROLINE HAD NEVER BEEN happier. The only blight was how she'd deceived her parents and how disappointed they would be. She might never see her father look at her with his loving smile again. Moreover, they might instruct her brothers to shun her, too.

Yet she would have her heart's desire by her side. She would be Geoffrey's wife and hopefully, one day, mother to his children. They both wanted a large family if they were so blessed. They'd had so much time to confirm their compatibility during the hours of travel, she was amazed at how perfectly they suited.

And the night before, after dinner, he'd taken her innocence gently and given her pleasure in return. After another long day of travel, with the Scottish border growing ever closer, she was looking forward to another night of passion.

"You ate your dinner rather quickly," he teased once they were alone in their chamber. Already, he was helping her to undress.

"As did you," she said, letting him pull her gown over her head, not feeling the least shyness now when she stood before him in her shift. When that last barrier was slid off her shoulders and down her breasts, her nipples stiffened.

"You are so beautiful," he said, reaching out to brush his knuckles over each peaked bud.

"There are many beautiful women in the world," she said.

"I love only one," he promised. "And if all you had to recommend you was your beauty, I would not have fallen in love with you, but if you had no beauty at all, I vow I would love you as much as I do now. Caroline Chimes, you have captured my heart and own it entirely."

Her cheeks heated. "You sound more like a poet every day."

"Indeed, you have brought out the romantic side of me. But also, the animal side." Without warning, he scooped her into his arms and deposited her upon the bed.

She yelped and then laughed. "Hurry," she beseeched. "Undress and join me."

The night before, for her sake, he'd dimmed the lamps before they removed all their clothing, making it all the more sensual when they stroked each other's bare skin while preserving a modicum of modesty for her first time.

Tonight, she could see all of him, his hard planes and his muscular figure, the dusting of hair across his chest and legs, and his manhood jutting out and up.

"We are so different," she said with wonder.

He chuckled. "And for that, I thank God."

Once beside her, he claimed her mouth under his while stroking her sensitive skin. Circling her breasts first, he caressed lower, down her stomach.

When he tore his mouth away and bent lower to suck upon first one of her pink pearls, then the other, Caroline thought the bed was tilting beneath her. Arching back, closing her eyes, she gripped his shoulders, only to feel Geoffrey's hand slide lower. Unable to help her wanton behavior, she lifted her hips to meet his skilled fingers as at last he touched her core.

As happened the previous night, it took very little time for her to reach the utmost pleasure, her body tightening almost unbearably and then releasing all at once in a joyful, exquisite blossoming sensation.

Even before her heart ceased its frantic racing, he fitted his jutting arousal to her damp channel and surged inside her. Again, her hips lifted to meet his thrust.

"I love you," he reminded her.

"I love you," she echoed.

They said nothing more as he began a slow rhythm of desirable torture.

When she was panting with exertion, trying to reach the pinnacle again, he slipped his hand between their bodies to touch where she most throbbed.

"Yes," she hissed, then shattered beneath him into a thousand pieces of ecstasy.

With a guttural groan, he continued rocking, increasing the pace until his body tensed. While she felt him shudder under her fingertips, he released the warm proof of his fulfillment deep inside her.

When Geoffrey collapsed atop her before quickly rolling to the side and hugging her to him, she decided she wouldn't mind if they had a baby by next autumn. In fact, such a happy occurrence would please her immensely.

As she drifted off to sleep, she was thinking of names for their children, names that evoked the many facets of a diamond—clarity, purity, and brilliance.

CHAPTER FOURTEEN

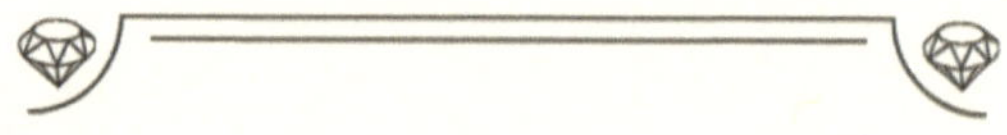

"Ha! Caught you." James didn't know how Chimes could have been so quick, but the earl had beaten him to the start of the Great North Road and then kept on going, albeit at a slower pace.

"I told you I had a rum prancer," Chimes said. "If I'd known you were going to ride a miserable rip like that, I would have insisted we journey separately. At the very least, I would have lent you some respectable horse flesh."

It was an idiotic insult since they both rode thoroughbreds. James dug his heels in, and his horse surged forward. For a furlong he raced Chimes, neck and neck, until they realized the futility.

"You know we'll be switching horses constantly, and thus, it's ridiculous to argue who has the best mount. We're wasting any endurance they may have at any rate."

"True," Chimes said, easing up.

James did the same. The best part about this type of exhausting, determined gait was it was nearly impossible to talk more than a short quip every once in a while. Thus, they lapsed into silence until the time came to switch out their horses in four hours at a coaching inn.

"If we keep this up and ride through the night, we may even get to Gretna before them."

"YOU WERE GOING TO LEAVE me behind," Lady Chimes insisted, taking the empty backward-facing seat and setting her bag beside her on the fine leather squab.

Marianne Diamond, who had climbed in first and taken her preferred place, could only shrug. Lady Chimes was correct. After telling James she wished he hadn't pushed them together, she'd kissed him goodbye at midnight and then decided to travel alone.

If Lady Chimes hadn't returned to the Diamond home at dawn as the maid and footman were packing the traveling coach, Marianne would have given a rude salute when she passed by the street upon which the Chimes lived and not bothered to collect her.

Yet before she could head out, Lady Chimes had arrived with a trunk, a leather bag, and a basket of food. And Marianne was trapped with the infernal woman for God only knew how many hours.

"Since we are as different as chalk and cheese," she said, "why don't we maintain a polite silence unless absolutely necessary?"

"Fine with me," Lady Chimes agreed, drawing needlepoint out of her bag.

Hating to do needle work herself, still, Marianne stared with fascination at what a hash the other woman was making of it and longed to point out there were more knots and holes than actual proper stitches. Not that she could do any better.

Pulling out a brand-new book, *The Inheritance* by Mrs. Ferrier, she set it on her lap, fully intending to delve in. For a moment, she thought what wicked fun it would have been to have brought Mrs. Ferrier's previous novel, simply titled *Marriage*, and left it in view of her carriage companion, to vex her.

In any case, after staring unseeingly out the window for a long while, Marianne closed her eyes, lulled by the rocking of the carriage.

"IT'S GOING TO BE TOO late," Geoffrey said, squeezing Caroline's hand as they crossed the River Sark after the sun had set. "It's called an 'irregular marriage,' but I don't fancy stumbling around Gretna Green in the darkness looking for someone to wed us."

"Nor I." Caroline shivered beside him. On the carriage floor, the hot bricks from the morning had long grown cold as marble. "It's far too brisk to do anything tonight except sit by a warm and perfectly regular fire."

"We'll stay at the King's Head. It's right on the roadside, according to reports. I don't believe it is grand by any means, but someone there can marry us in the morning."

Sadly, Geoffrey was correct. From what he could see as they drove alongside, the hostelry had a very plain, even shabby façade. However, the chimneys were smoking, indicating some heat, and lamps shone through the lower two windows.

"Doesn't seem like the type of place to send in my footman and arrange a room," he said. "We'll go in together and see if it looks up to snuff."

He helped her down.

"The thought of returning to that chilly carriage makes the King's Head look most welcoming," Caroline said.

He'd learned she wasn't fussy or persnickety. Moreover, she could tolerate a great deal of inconvenience, whether gristly steak pie, a lumpy mattress, or a noisy tavern directly below their room.

They entered through the low doorway directly into a small passage. On the right was the pub room and on the left was a closed door. In front of them, a staircase disappeared into the unlit floor above.

The only saving grace was a cat seated at the foot of the stairs, which greeted them by rubbing against Caroline's ankles.

"At least there won't be mice," Geoffrey said, and they went into the barroom.

It wasn't joyless, but it wasn't bustling with happy locals either. At one of the small tables nearest the hearth sat a couple who looked down and away as if to hide their faces. The other tables were empty save one occupied in the far corner by people with their backs to the room. Geoffrey assumed it was the nature of a place that was infamous for hurried weddings—everyone would wish to keep their identities concealed.

A barman looked up from where he was reading a newspaper and nodded by way of greeting.

Geoffrey nodded back. "Do you have a room for us, and another for my two servants?"

"Aye," said the man.

Geoffrey wanted to ask if the room was clean, but seeing how Caroline was tired and the December weather frigid, they should settle in while they could.

"Can we get a meal, too?" he asked, wondering how far hospitality would extend in the stark little place.

The man looked past to the darkness outside as if determining the time, and then he sniffed and swung his head toward an open doorway behind him, which led to the back of the house.

"Mattie!" he yelled.

"Aye," called back a female voice.

"You got any stew left and bread?"

"Aye," she answered.

The barman faced them again.

"Aye, we can feed you."

"Only if we want stew," Geoffrey quipped.

The man didn't smile. Apparently, there was not much of a sense of humor in this dour little inn.

"Which we do," Caroline asserted, beginning to pull off her gloves.

"It's quite good," Geoffrey's father said.

His father!

Geoffrey gaped at the man who rose from the table in the corner, joined by Lord Chimes.

"Father!" Caroline exclaimed.

"No trouble in here," the barman warned, standing straight.

"No trouble," James Diamond agreed affably. "Merely a family reunion."

"Two reunions," Lord Chimes said. "And I don't know yet about trouble."

"Nonsense. Come, sit with us," Geoffrey's father invited. "Bring these travelers some stew," he said to the barman.

"And red wine," Geoffrey added, feeling Caroline trembling beside him. They crossed the small room and, surprisingly, Lord Chimes grasped his daughter's shoulders and drew her in for a hug.

"Your mother and I were worried," he told her, loudly enough for them all to hear.

Geoffrey felt like a cad for the first time since they'd fled London. Then before he could do so himself, her father drew out a chair for her.

In the next instant, to his astonishment, he found himself sitting with the two fathers as if it were the most normal thing in the world to be caught trying to elope.

"You made good time," Geoffrey said. "I imagine you didn't get any sleep."

"You are correct," his father said. "At least, not a full night. We wasted time looking for you at some of the inns along the way." With that statement, he glared at Lord Chimes.

"It's true I had hoped we would find you before you reached this god-forsaken place."

"Hear now!" said the barman who was delivering their bowls of stew and a basket of bread. "That's uncalled for."

"I meant the village, sir, not your fine establishment," Lord Chimes said.

"Wine," Geoffrey croaked, making a desperate drinking motion with his hand.

"Coming up," the man said and departed.

"We looked in some of the more likely coaching inns," James Diamond continued. "And then we gave up and rode like the devil was after us. We've been here for hours." He looked pleased with himself.

"What if we hadn't come in here," Geoffrey asked.

"We've paid people in all the nearby hotels to keep an eye open for you."

"There's only two others," Lord Chimes said. Then he fixed Geoffrey with a hard stare.

"In truth, you're lucky you made it this far. If I'd found my daughter with you in one of those inns, I would have taken her directly home," Lord Chimes said.

Then he looked at Caroline. "You're awfully quiet, Daughter. What do you have to say for yourself?"

Geoffrey watched her take a deep breath, visibly sit taller, and then address her father with confidence.

"I am quite pleased to be marrying Lord Diamond no matter the how and the where of it. I hope you won't try to stop us. You cannot do so, here in Scotland."

"Only with my pistol," Lord Chimes threatened.

Geoffrey startled and saw his father straighten, too. He had no doubt whose side his father would be on should violence erupt.

"Father!" Caroline admonished. "The law is on our side."

"Speaking in jest," Lord Chimes grumbled. "Merely in jest."

"We plan to marry in the morning and head straight back to London," Geoffrey explained to the man who would be his father-in-law.

He wished he could add that he hadn't laid a finger on Caroline and had waited for her to become his lawful wife. Yet such restraint had proven impossible.

"You cannot marry," Lord Chimes said.

Geoffrey looked to his father for support but found none.

"As much as I hate to agree with Chimes on anything he says, he is correct," Lord Diamond said. "You cannot. And if we have to use force to stop you, we will."

CHAPTER FIFTEEN

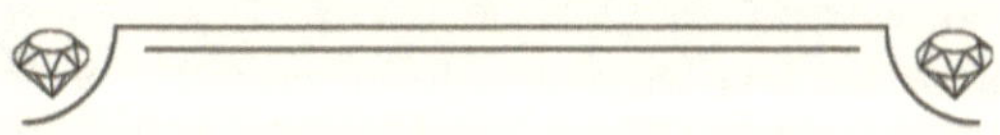

"**I** love him," Caroline declared. She glanced at Geoffrey, and he winked, giving her strength. "As deeply as you love Mother," she said to her father. And then she addressed her would-be father-in-law. "And as assuredly as you love Lady Diamond."

The barman took that moment to deliver a carafe of ruby-red wine and two glasses. With haste born of the tension that had Caroline's nerves stretched taut, Geoffrey poured them each a full glass, and they drank a hardy sip.

"That may be, Lady Caroline," said the Earl Diamond, "but you cannot marry tomorrow morning. You cannot marry my son until his mother and your mother arrive."

Caroline's mouth dropped slightly open before she regained her composure.

"My mother is coming? Here?"

"With *my* mother?" Geoffrey asked. "Together?"

"In the same carriage," her father assured her.

"Impossible," Caroline murmured, thinking she would have to see the two women descend from the same coach to believe it.

"When they arrive, which may be by the end of tomorrow if they followed the same path as you, then we shall have one of these anvil weddings," Lord Diamond said.

Her father shook his head slowly. "It might be better to get one of the innkeepers to do it." They all turned as one to look at the barman who was blowing his nose on a rag and drinking what appeared to be a large glass of whisky.

"Or some type of *official* person, if not an actual vicar," her father continued. "Your mother will have a fit if you let a blacksmith marry you."

Caroline considered all the demands her mother might make when she arrived. The wedding could be delayed for days if not weeks.

"This is why we eloped," she protested. "We are not supposed to wait for family or worry about the officiator. Next thing, Mother will arrive and want to order a special gown."

"You should have traveled as quickly as Diamond and I did if you wanted to elope without interference," her father said, "not dillydallying up the countryside, stopping each night."

As he said the last word, his gaze turned to Geoffrey. His expression became a scowl. "I'm sure you had separate rooms for the journey."

Caroline pressed her lips together, but Geoffrey swallowed his wine in a gulp and began to cough, spluttering the wooden table with droplets. His father reached around and began to pound his back until he held up his hand.

She was glad when Geoffrey said nothing. It was better not to respond than to offer an outright lie.

"There is nothing for it," she said, changing the subject. "We shall have to wait for the ladies. Hopefully, the weather remains clear. Now, I shall eat my stew and get a good night's sleep, for I vow I have barely—" she cut herself off.

What a ninny! She nearly told both the fathers how little sleep she'd had the past two nights. *And how would she explain that?*

"Both inns were extremely loud," Geoffrey said into the awkward silence.

"A good thing this one seems perfectly quiet," her father said tightly, continuing to glare at Geoffrey.

Caroline felt the heat rush to her cheeks. She could never have imagined sitting at a table with three noblemen, one of whom was her father, with the prattle being about her sleeping or not sleeping, as the case had been.

Another mortifying moment occurred when they retired. The barman led her and Geoffrey upstairs to a room. A single room.

"I told you," Geoffrey said, "we need two."

"You said the other was for your servants," the man protested. "In any case, this is the last one, and both your trunks have been put inside by your footman."

"My son will sleep with me," Lord Diamond said, averting disaster. "Grab your case."

Hurrying to avoid the sight of their trunks resting side by side taking up all the floor space, Geoffrey hefted it into his arms. She stood aside so he could exit the small room.

"Goodnight, Lady Caroline," he said politely as if they'd never been entwined naked in each other's arms. And he disappeared from view around her father, who stood with his arms crossed in the hall.

Just like that, without even being able to give Geoffrey a kiss, she found herself alone in the room where a single lamp had been lit and three small chunks of coal were smoldering.

"I'm in the room directly beside yours," her father said as a warning more than to reassure her of her safety. Then he closed the door on her astonished face.

As it turned out, she slept like the dead after stripping off her outer garments and climbing into the soft bed in her shift. However, in the morning, two astonishing things happened.

"Did you see the snow?" she asked Geoffrey, who was seated in the room across from where they'd eaten the night before. The hearth was glowing, and he was the only one there, reading an old newspaper and drinking tea.

He rose to his feet upon her entrance.

"I couldn't miss it. There was a large gap in the window glazing in our room, and the snow started blowing in last night before we stuffed my father's handkerchief in the hole."

"It's beautiful," she exclaimed with a sigh.

"Not when it's on your counterpane," he said. "Besides, the only beauty I see is you."

With that, she walked directly into his outstretched arms, and they shared a kiss. Her body tingled when his mouth touched hers, and she couldn't help pressing close.

"A fine sight for a father to see on Christmas Eve."

Belatedly, they sprang apart. With cheeks flaming, she faced her father.

"Seeing your daughter in love should be a fine sight, indeed," she told him. Then she realized what he'd said. "Christmas Eve! Is it?"

She looked at Geoffrey. "I hadn't realized."

He appeared equally astonished. "Nor I. I suppose we had our minds on other matters, and the month slipped away."

Lord Diamond came in looking concerned. "I may head out to find the ladies. They should still be about five hours away. The snow has stopped, so I doubt they will get stuck anywhere, but I don't want to risk it."

"I'll go with you," her father said.

She felt a tingle of anticipation. She and Geoffrey would be left alone again. By the quick smile upon his handsome face, he realized the same thing, quelling it just as quickly when their fathers stopped discussing their travel plans.

"We'll trust you to remain here," Lord Diamond said.

"And unwed," her father added.

"Of course," Geoffrey answered. "I would offer to go, too, but I don't want to leave Lady Caroline alone in this place."

"Hear now!" said the barman as he brought in tea service. "That's uncalled for," he repeated his words from the night before, sounding as if he were used to having his establishment slighted. "We have no trouble in this inn."

"You have a broken window," Lord Diamond said, "giving us a chilly night."

The man's eyebrows rose, but he set down the plain wooden tea tray. "We'll put some wax paper on it if you're staying another night."

"I believe we are," Lord Diamond said.

The barman rubbed his hands. "Don't usually have our rooms all filled for two nights in a row by the same folks." And he wandered off, presumably to tell Mattie in the kitchen the good news.

"I'll have a cup of tea," her father said, "and one of those scones before we go."

Lord Diamond shrugged, but in two minutes, all four of them, including both the fathers, were tucking into scones with cream and thistle jelly.

Caroline wondered how terribly disloyal it would be if she and Geoffrey married and left as soon as the men went in search of their wives.

And then a third astonishing thing happened. The front door of the inn opened, and the two mothers blew in along with a frigid gust. Caroline could see it all through the open sitting-room doorway.

"Mother!" she exclaimed, jumping up, causing the three men to do the same.

The two ladies turned in amazement and stumbled into the room.

"Isn't this a fine how-do-you-do!" Caroline's mother exclaimed. "We're out in the brutal elements, and they're all inside here warm as toast. And eating it, too."

They all started talking at once.

"Did they marry?" Lady Diamond asked.

"How did you get here so quickly?" Lord Chimes asked.

"Did you stop them?" Lady Chimes asked.

"Are the horses in good condition?" Lord Diamond wondered.

"Would you like tea?" Caroline offered.

"Is this the best inn in the area?" Lady Diamond asked, looking around.

"Hush," Geoffrey said. That made the four parents stop and stare at him with varying degrees of annoyance. "Please, ladies, won't you sit and warm up? We'll get more tea and scones."

At the commotion, the barman wandered in. "I don't have any more rooms," he said, rubbing his hands with glee at being full up. "But I'll bring more tea and my wife's scones."

"We won't need more rooms," Lord Diamond said. "These ladies are with us."

Caroline considered that statement. They certainly would not need another room if she and Geoffrey married that very day.

"My father and Lord Diamond were about to head out and find you, thinking you still hours away."

Her mother made a face, and Lady Diamond raised a perfect eyebrow.

"It looked to me as though they were stuffing their potato traps, not the least bit worried over us," the latter said.

"How did you get here so quickly?" Lord Chimes repeated his question while he dragged more chairs to the table.

"We didn't stop the second night. The innkeeper's wife had an elbow for weather, and she said—"

"I beg your pardon," Geoffrey's father interrupted. "Did you say an elbow for weather?"

"Yes," Lady Diamond said. "Her elbow twinges when snow is imminent."

"And it was twinging," Lady Chimes agreed. "We ate our supper and continued on with fresh horses."

"But how did you find us here?" Geoffrey asked.

"Your carriage is parked directly across on the square. I hope no one steals it."

"Hear now!" said the barman, who was carrying in another tea tray, piled high with scones and jam.

"That's uncalled for," Caroline, Geoffrey, and the two fathers said at the same time as the barman.

The ladies looked at all of them as if they were lunatics.

"If we'd stayed at the last inn," Lady Diamond said once she had a cup of tea in hand, "we might have spent our Christmas Eve and Christmas Day trapped there, too."

"How brave of you," Lord Diamond said, looking fondly at his wife before taking another bite of warm scone.

"Never mind that," Caroline's mother snapped. "Are these young people married?"

Caroline's father answered. "We told them they couldn't do so until you arrived."

Her mother pursed her lips and shook her head while Lady Diamond observed her with interest. Hopefully, she wouldn't mind having Caroline for a daughter-in-law.

"Do you condone this marriage now?" her mother asked her father.

Caroline held her breath.

CHAPTER SIXTEEN

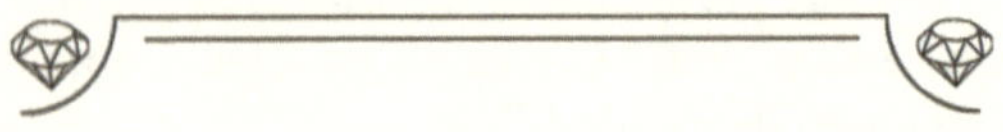

Caroline felt Geoffrey take her hand and give it a reassuring squeeze. What's more, he did it in front of everyone. Whatever her parents and his parents said, she knew they would marry, even if they had to run away again, farther into Scotland.

"We are too late for condoning," Lord Diamond pronounced.

"Or for prohibiting," her father added. "Our daughter has spent three days alone traveling with this man. They must marry. I think we all know that now."

Caroline felt a twinge in her stomach, and it had nothing to do with the miracle of snow. Mortification, embarrassment, a little shame over causing their parents to come such a long way chasing after them—*were she and Geoffrey selfish?*

She glanced up at him, and the warm sparkle in his eyes quashed all her doubts. They were in love after all.

"Very well," her mother said. "Allow Lady Diamond and I to get our feet under us, and then we shall bear witness to the marriage of our children."

Caroline was surprised to see Geoffrey's mother nodding. "Agreed," Lady Diamond said. "Do they have chocolate here, by the way? Or only tea?"

AFTER ALL THE HULLABALOO, the actual anvil ceremony was almost humdrum. Geoffrey was pleased to have the entire authentic experience once the mothers agreed to the location. The King's Head barman said he could do the proceedings if pressed, but referred them to the best officiator, the smithy next to the road in the very center of Gretna Green.

Thus, around two o'clock, the party of six strolled from the inn across the grassy green to the blacksmith's shop. The apprentice was the first to greet them, and he went to find Mr. Lang, who appeared in his heavy apron in the open doorway.

"Will you marry them?" asked Lord Chimes, nodding toward Geoffrey and Caroline.

The man grinned to see an entire wedding party when usually he was faced with only a harried couple, looking fearfully over their shoulders.

"Aye, if you've got the coin."

Geoffrey was astonished when Caroline's father did, indeed, pay the blacksmith, handing over two guineas and earning a kiss on his cheek from his grateful daughter. They entered the hot, almost stifling workroom.

And then the man asked them their names as he and Caroline stood before him holding hands. Mr. Lang even managed to bring a little formality to the absurdly brief ceremony, mentioning God and trust and long happiness before proclaiming them man and wife.

When the blacksmith told them they could kiss, Geoffrey thought it would be the most uncomfortable thing he'd done in his whole life. Moreover, it might earn him Lord and Lady Chimes's fury. Regardless, as soon as he locked gazes with Caroline, she smiled up at him. In front of all those watching, he gave her a brief but firm kiss.

Then Mr. Lang lifted a hammer resting at the wooden base, which held an anvil, and gave the iron a mighty whack.

"The sound will tell the whole village another couple has married," the man said. Then he handed each of them a calling card. "Tell your friends of my easy, swift, affordable service."

With that, he walked away, unconcerned about their signing a register. Regardless, the apprentice provided a half-sheet of paper, a "certificate," he called it proudly, which he said they could put their names on as well as those of their witnesses. Then he, too, disappeared.

Geoffrey glanced down. "The blacksmith can write, apparently. He has signed his name." He handed this to his father.

"Simon," Lord Diamond exclaimed. He started to laugh. "My boy, heir to an earldom, has just been wed by a Simple Simon."

Lord Chimes didn't look so amused. "As long as it's legal." He peered at the card in his hand before shoving it into his pocket. "Tell our friends! Hardly."

The mothers were silent. Then each sniffed and withdrew a handkerchief, wiping their noses and dabbing at their eyes. It might be because the building was hot as Hades, but more likely, sentimentality had overcome each of them.

"Lady Chimes, please don't cry," Geoffrey said. "I have gained a second mother, and I vow never to give your daughter a moment's grief. I shall make her as happy as I am able."

The lady nodded before hugging her daughter and then taking her husband's hand.

Geoffrey's father slapped him on the shoulder, and Lady Diamond actually hugged Caroline.

"Welcome to the Diamond family."

"Thank you, my lady. I hope to be a worthy member."

Lord Chimes, who was still within earshot, let out a loud snort of derision.

Before any unpleasantness could arise, Geoffrey said, "I think it would be a good idea to cross back over into

England and lodge at the closest coaching inn before dark. One that has a bit of luxury to it. The Crown and Blade, perhaps."

With everyone in agreement, they returned to the King's Head and packed up, much to the disappointment of the barman.

"For the first time, I am helping you into our carriage as my wife," Geoffrey said to Caroline, who hadn't stopped beaming since he'd kissed her at the blacksmith's.

She offered a squeak of excitement and settled in on the same side as him. The bricks had been warmed, they had a woolen blanket over their laps, and a flask of brandy. Their mothers had been joined by their fathers in the earl's coach with the horses tied up to follow.

"I am extremely glad not to be in my father's carriage," he said. "I cannot imagine how thick the silence, nor conversely how tense the conversation."

"And to think, we brought about their new friendship," she said teasingly.

He laughed. In the next instant, she'd twisted to face him and put her arms around him.

"That was a tepid kiss at Simple Simon's, dear husband. I think we can do better."

LONG BEFORE SUNSET, THEY reached the Crown and Blade. A celebratory meal was ordered, and the three married couples were assigned their rooms.

"I don't care if we were given the smallest room of the three," Caroline said. "We only need room for the bed."

"You are a wanton wife," Geoffrey said, "and I would strip you now had we time. Being without you last night was torture. But our parents will be waiting in the dining room."

"I'm sure they are already drinking wine and won't notice if we're a little late. In fact, isn't it expected?"

"I believe you are the wiser of the two of us, Lady Diamond. In fact, you would be expected to change from that pretty gown into something less delicate."

"Daphne was an angel to loan it to me, but no one saw it under my redingote."

"I see it now, and you are the loveliest bride I could ever imagine."

"Thank you. But undress me quickly."

With the hearth already glowing, warming their small room, Geoffrey removed all her layers until she stood bare before him in the rosy light.

"What is my excuse for appearing downstairs in different clothing?" he asked, shedding his jacket and waistcoat before tearing off his cravat.

She sighed. "No excuse is needed. You are a new husband. And if you don't touch me this instant, you will have broken your promise to keep me always happy."

She took the two steps to the bed, which sported a thick mattress, puffy with down. Scrambling onto it, she gave him a delightful view of her rear end.

He stepped out of his trousers, nearly tripping in his haste, and joined her. First a thorough kiss, with dancing tongues and sighs of relief at having made it exactly where they wanted to be.

Then he ran his finger across her nipple which pearled, begging him to kiss it. He complied.

"Are you truly mine to love and pleasure for the rest of our lives?" He could hardly believe it.

"I am. But we must make love hastily at this moment and can do it again more languidly after dinner."

"As I said before, you are the wiser of the two of us." He covered her body, settling between her thighs.

In a short while, they reached the pinnacle of their passion together.

As they were dressing, Caroline said, "I half expected my mother to knock on the door and ask what was taking us so long."

"That would have diminished my ardor considerably," Geoffrey told her.

"I confess I am more comfortable in a thicker weave. And I am exceedingly grateful we don't have to go any farther than the dining room tonight. Will you do up the buttons, please?"

"I am already turned into a lady's maid," he teased.

"Is it every husband's dread?"

"Not this husband," Geoffrey vowed. "I am honored. Glad you didn't accept either of those young men I saw you with in the autumn, one at the theatre and the other at the park."

Furrowing her brow, Caroline considered, and then she widened her eyes.

"Oh, sweet husband. I hate to tell you this, but you were jealous of my own brothers."

Stunned, Geoffrey considered.

"Then I guess I should be glad they didn't ride to Scotland, too. They might have been less understanding than your parents."

"Truly. My eldest brother might still wish to punch you in the nose for eloping with me. I suppose they are having Christmas alone this year."

"They'll blame me for that, too."

"Probably."

"Before I get into any more trouble," Geoffrey suggested, "let's go down to dinner."

AFTER A SUMPTUOUS CHRISTMAS repast of two soups and sixteen dishes, including doe-venison and goose, a roasted vegetable dish of parsnips, potatoes, and leeks, and poached pears and walnuts with fresh cream, their party of six sat with three empty carafes of wine on the table.

With their stomachs bulging, the Diamonds and the Chimes began to bicker.

"What was the wretched wager?" Lady Chimes demanded of her husband. "Didn't this rascal," she jerked a thumb at Lord Diamond, "try to make you claim *his* wife was the most beautiful woman in London?"

"What!" exclaimed Lady Diamond. "I never heard of such a thing. It would be vulgar, no matter its veracity."

"In fact," Lord Chimes said, already red-cheeked, "the scoundrel tried to get me to claim that *you*, my lady wife, were *not* the most beautiful woman."

Lady Chimes's mouth worked as she considered. "Are you saying you lost the wager because you wouldn't disparage me?"

"When Diamond set up the wager and said he would name the most beautiful woman in London and that I couldn't disprove it, how could I know he would name my own wife? But he was correct, I couldn't disprove it. I couldn't lie," Lord Chimes said. "You are the most beautiful woman, not just in London, but in all of England, as far as I'm concerned. Before a room full of our peers, I wouldn't gainsay him. Thus, I paid my debt."

"You thought I would name my own wife, I suppose," Lord Diamond said, looking far too delighted at having outfoxed the other man.

"Any honorable man would have done so," Lord Chimes stated, wiping the glee off the other man's face.

Lady Diamond's expression was furious as she rounded on her husband. "In front of all the men at White's, you declared Lady Chimes to be the most beautiful woman."

"In *London*," Lord Diamond corrected. "And you were at our country home in Derbyshire." He let that sink in.

Meanwhile, Lady Chimes had moved closer to her own husband. "Then you didn't wish you had ended up with her?" She jerked her head toward Geoffrey's mother.

Lord Chimes appeared shocked. "Of course not. She's vain, fickle, and flighty."

"I say!" Lady Diamond interrupted.

"Indeed," Lord Diamond added, setting down his glass and leaning toward Lord Chimes. "You must apologize for such slander at once."

"Oh no, dear husband," Lady Diamond said. "He speaks the truth but still! He didn't have to say it so boldly."

"Indeed," said Lord Diamond again. "Apologize to my wife for stating the truth so boldly and in mixed company, too. She may be vain, fickle, and flighty, but she's perfect for me."

Lady Diamond started to laugh. "I'm glad to hear that." And then her husband draped his arm around her.

Lord and Lady Chimes stared at them as if they were in a madhouse. But then, the lady had another question for her husband.

"So, you don't hate Diamond for taking *her* away from you?"

"No, I hate him because he swindled me out of a goodly sum with his tricky wager."

"Well, do you loathe Lady Diamond for going with him?" Lady Chimes persisted.

"Again, no. I'm glad she went with him because it opened the way for me to find you. But why do *you* hate him?" Lord Chimes demanded of his wife.

"I don't really," she confessed, "only for your sake, dearest. I thought he'd pricked your pride and was a dishonorable dog to boot."

Lady Diamond patted her husband's cheek. "He's not a dog, but he's no saint, either. After all, he did lead me down the garden path," she pointed out. "I never had a blemish upon my reputation before."

This caused Lord Diamond to break out into whoops of laughter that instantly snatched the affectionate expression from Lady Diamond's face.

Ignoring them both, Lady Chimes spoke only to her husband. "Anyway, it was *her* I hated because I thought she had won your heart before I ever had the chance."

"No, my love. From the moment I saw you, I knew you were meant to be mine."

Finally, Geoffrey spoke up. "That is precisely how I felt when I first saw Lady Caroline. That is, when I first bumped into her."

"And I, when I saw him," she admitted. "I didn't know he was meant to be mine exactly, but I felt a sizzle of interest to discover if I wanted him to be mine."

"And did you?" he asked.

"Most certainly, I did."

Not a single one of their parents was bothering to listen.

"But after our long journey together," Lady Diamond said, "we don't hate one another anymore."

Lady Chimes frowned. "Why did *you* hate me?"

"Because you so easily took my place with Lord Chimes, as if I didn't matter. Also, because you're a mushroom."

"Shall we take a stroll outside and discuss our future?" Geoffrey asked her.

"It's rather frosty out," she reminded him. "Perhaps we could stroll inside the inn instead. Or maybe we could simply retire for the night."

By her sparkling gaze, he knew they would find something interesting to do in their small but plush room. Offering her his arm, which she took, they left behind their parents, still squabbling and discussing the distant past.

He didn't care. All he cared about was having fulfilled his goal for the year, finding and marrying the most perfect woman!

EPILOGUE

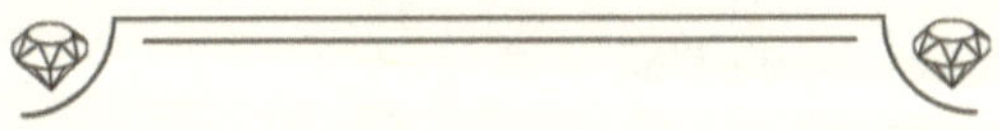

"Are you awake?" Caroline whispered.

Geoffrey yawned and rolled over, seeing her green eyes open and her glorious red hair spread out upon the pillow. He grinned.

"We just had our first full night in bed as husband and wife," he said, as if it was a revelation she might not have realized.

She nodded. "And it's Christmas day. How did we forget?"

"I guess we had other things on our minds." He still did, and he started to reach for her.

"Luckily, I have a gift for you, something I was working on in the carriage during our journey to Gretna Green. I thought up a poem and memorized it."

"I thought you were sleeping quite a bit. I didn't realize someone could snore while dreaming up poetry."

She smacked his shoulder. "I do not snore. And I promise you, I was fashioning a poem. I haven't had a chance to write it down, but as your Christmas present, I shall recite it for you."

He drew the sheet and blanket down to expose her bare breasts.

"Go ahead." But one of his hands stroked the sensitive area at her waist, making her shiver.

She laughed. "You are being wicked and will make me forget my poetry."

"Very well. I will behave." He placed his palm on her stomach, then brushed back and forth with the pad of his thumb, which was even more distracting.

Taking a breath, she began:

"Like Romeo and Juliet, we were thwarted from the start.
Yet unlike her, I shall not end with a dagger in my heart."

Geoffrey startled at her choice of words. "Caroline, that's rather—"

"*Shh*, I'm not finished!" She cleared her throat and continued.

"At first, I wondered 'wherefore art thou Diamond?'
A name I was not allowed to love nor to dance."

"You can't dance with a name," he pointed out, feeling the hint of laughter stirring inside him. She shook her head to silence him.

"What's in a name? I asked. By any other, you would still smell like a rose."

He bit his lower lip wanting to giggle.

"And for the rest of my life, my full heart will happily prance."

"Stop, please," he begged. Her poem was so awful he knew he would be unable to hold in his laughter any longer.

"But there is much more," Caroline protested. "Don't you want to hear about my boundless love? The more I have, the more I give to you for both are infinite."

He chuckled. "You just mangled one of Shakespeare's best lines."

She blinked innocently, then she shrugged. "I couldn't possibly say it any better. I was teasing you. I really was sleeping in the carriage."

"Thank God. Your poem was dreadful."

"I'll say only this—I am glad you stumbled into me at the Fenwicks' ball."

"'They stumble that run fast,' said the Bard's Friar Lawrence."

Scrunching up her nose, Caroline shook her head. "I don't think that applies, or at least, I hope not."

He leaned over and placed a kiss on the gentle curve of her stomach.

"I think you're correct. Our story is already faring much better than Romeo and Juliet's. Let's forget about them. Besides, I don't need anything more from you. You have presented me with the most wonderful gift already. Quite simply, you gave me yourself."

Again, he kissed her stomach, and while he was deciding whether to move up or down, he added, "I am the one who must think of what to give you on this special day."

She stroked his hair, her fingers threading through it, tugging gently.

"Dearest husband, how many women can say they received a Diamond for Christmas? I need nothing else."

He began to kiss a trail along her body.

"On the other hand," she said, her breath catching in her throat when his tongue touched her, "it would be rude of me to turn down your generosity."

"Merry Christmas, Wife."

"Merry Christmas, Husband."

Finis

ABOUT THE AUTHOR

USA Today bestselling author Sydney Jane Baily writes historical romance set in Victorian England, late 19th-century America, the Middle Ages, the Georgian era, and the Regency period. She believes in happily-ever-after stories, engaging characters, and passionate romance with a touch of intrigue.

Born and raised in California, she has traveled the world, spending a lot of exceedingly happy time in the U.K. where her extended family resides, eating fish and chips, drinking shandy, and snacking on Maltesers and Cadbury bars. Sydney currently lives in New England with her family—human, canine, and feline.

At her website, SydneyJaneBaily.com, you can learn more about her books, sign up for her newsletter (and get a free book), and contact her. She loves to hear from her readers.

www.ingramcontent.com/pod-product-compliance
Lightning Source LLC
Chambersburg PA
CBHW030902200726
48289CB00003B/860